He had prayed for
a vision of the new God—
and was answered. . . .

A great clear light formed in the sky above him. Tibor peeped, half blinded, shielded his eyes with the terminal of his left manual gripper. . . . He could make out features on its surface: eyes, a mouth, ears, tangled hair. The mouth was screaming at him.

"You mock at me! See what I can do to save you if I wish. How easy it is. Pray!" the face demanded. "On your hands and knees!"

"But," Tibor said, "I have no hands or knees."

All at once, Tibor found himself lifted upward, then set down hard on the grass. Legs. He was kneeling. Only the God of Wrath could do what had just been achieved.

"Pray!" the face instructed. "Pray!"

**Dangerous Visions
by the Master of Future Paranoia**

DEUS IRAE

Philip K. Dick
&
Roger Zelazny

A DELL BOOK

Published by
DELL PUBLISHING CO., INC.
1 Dag Hammarskjold Plaza
New York, N.Y. 10017

Dell ® TM 681510, Dell Publishing Co., Inc.

ISBN: 0-440-11838-7

Reprinted by arrangement with
Doubleday & Company, Inc.

Printed in the United States of America

Previous Dell Edition
Two printings
New Dell Edition
First printing—October 1980

This novel, in loving memory, is dedicated to *Stanley G. Weinbaum,* for his having given the world his story *"A Martian Odyssey."*

ONE

Here! The black-spotted cow drawing the bicycle cart. In the center of the cart. And at the doorway of the sacristy Father Handy glanced against the morning sunlight from Wyoming to the north as if the sun came from that direction, saw the church's employee, the limbless trunk with knobbed head lolling as if in tripfantastic to a slow jig as the Holstein cow wallowed forward.

A bad day, Father Handy thought. For he had to declare bad news to Tibor McMasters. Turning, he reentered the church and hid himself; Tibor, on his cart, had not seen him, for Tibor hung in the clutch of withinthoughts and nausea; it always came to this when the artist appeared to begin his work: he was sick at his stomach, and any smell, any sight, even that of his own work, made him cough. And Father Handy wondered about this, the repellency of sense-reception early in the day, as if Tibor, he thought, does not want to be alive again another day.

He himself, the priest; he enjoyed the sun. The smell of hot, large clover from the surrounding pastures of Charlottesville, Utah. The tink-tink of the tags of the cows . . . he sniffed the air as it filled his church and yet—not the sight of Tibor but the awareness of the limbless man's pain; that caused him worry.

There, behind the altar, the miniscule part of the

work which had been accomplished; five years it would take Tibor, but time did not matter in a subject of this sort: through eternity—no, Father Handy thought; not eternity, because this thing is man-made and hence cursed—but for ages, it will be here generations. The other armless, legless persons to arrive later, who would not, could not, genuflect because they lacked the physiological equipment; this was accepted officially.

"Uuuuuuuub," the Holstein lowed, as Tibor, through his U.S. ICBM extensor system, reined it to a halt in the rear yard of the church, where Father Handy kept his detired, unmoving 1976 Cadillac, within which small lovely chickens, all feathered in gay gold, luminous, because they were Mexican banties, clung nightlong, bespoiling . . . and yet, why not? The dung of handsome birds that roamed in a little flock, led by Herbert G, the rooster who had flung himself up ages ago to confront all his rivals, won out and lived to be followed; a leader of beasts, Father Handy thought moodily. Inborn quality in Herbert G, who, right now, scratched within the succulent garden for bugs. For special mutant fat ones.

He, the priest, hated bugs, too many odd kinds, thrust up overnight from the fal't . . . so he loved the predators who fed on the chitinous crawlers, loved his flock of—amusing to think of—birds! Not men.

But men arrived, at least on the Holy Day, Tuesday—to differentiate it (purposefully) from the archaic Christian Holy Day, Sunday.

In the hind yard, Tibor detached his cart from the cow. Then, on battery power, the cart rolled up its special wood-plank ramp and into the church; Father Handy felt it within the building, the arrival of the man without limbs, who, retching, fought to control his abridged body so that he could resume work where he had left off at sunset yesterday.

To Ely, his wife, Father Handy said, "Do you have hot coffee for him? Please."

"Yes," she said, dry, dutiful, small, and withered, as if wetless personally; he disliked her body drabness as he watched her lay out a Melmac cup and saucer, not with love but with the unwarmed devotion of a priest's wife, therefore a priest's servant.

"Hi!" Tibor called cheerfully. Always, as if professionally, merry, above his physiological retching and reretching.

"Black," Father Handy said. "Hot. Right here." He stood aside so that the cart, which was massive for an indoor construct, could roll on through the corridor and into the church's kitchen.

"Morning, Mrs. Handy," Tibor said.

Ely Handy said dustily as she did not face the limbless man, "Good morning, Tibor. Pax be with you and with thy saintly spark."

"Pax or pox?" Tibor said, and winked at Father Handy.

No answer; the woman puttered. Hate, Father Handy thought, can take marvelous exceeding attenuated forms; he all at once yearned for it direct, open and ripe and directed properly. Not this mere lack of grace, this formality . . . he watched her get milk from the cooler.

Tibor began the difficult task of drinking coffee.

First he needed to make his cart stationary. He locked the simple brake. Then detached the selenoid-controlled relay from the ambulatory circuit and sent power from the liquid-helium battery to the manual circuit. A clean aluminum tubular extension reached out and at its terminal a six-digit gripping mechanism, each unit wired separately back through the surge-gates and to the shoulder muscles of the limbless man, groped for the empty cup; then, as Tibor saw it was still empty, he looked inquiringly.

"On the stove," Ely said, meaningly smiling.

So the cart's brake had to be unlocked; Tibor rolled to the stove, relocked the cart's brake once more via the selenoid selector-relays, and sent his manual grippers to lift the pot. The aluminum tubular extensor, armlike, brought the pot up tediously, in a near Parkinson-motion, until, finally, Tibor managed, through all the elaborate ICBM guidance components, to pour coffee into his cup.

Father Handy said, "I won't join you because I had pyloric spasms last night and when I got up this morning." He felt irritable, physically. Like you, he thought, I am, although a Complete, having trouble with my body this morning: with glands and hormones. He lit a cigarette, his first of the day, tasted the loose genuine tobacco, puffed, and felt much better; one chemical checked the overproduction of another, and now he seated himself at the table as Tibor, smiling cheerfully still, drank the heated-over coffee without complaint.

And yet—

Sometimes physical pain is a precognition of wicked things about to come, Father Handy thought, and in your case; is that it, do you know what I shall—must—tell you today? No choice, because what am I, if not a man-worm who is told; who, on Tuesday, tells, but this is only one day, and just an hour of that day.

"Tibor," he said, *"wie geht es Heute?"*

"Es geht mir gut," Tibor responded instantly.

They mutually loved their recollection and their use of German. It meant Goethe and Heine and Schiller and Kafka and Falada; both men, together, lived for this and on this. Now, since the work would soon come, it was a ritual, bordering on the sacred, a reminder of the after-daylight hours when the painting proved impossible and they could—had to—merely talk. In the semigloom of the kerosene lanterns and the firelight, which was a bad light source; too irregular, and Tibor had complained, in his understating way, of eye fatigue. And that was a dreadful harbinger, because nowhere in the Wyoming-Utah area could a lensman be found; no refractive glasswork had been lately possible, at least as near as Father Handy knew.

It would require a Pilg to get glasses for Tibor, if that became necessary; he blenched from that, because so often the church employee dragooned for a Pilg set off and never returned. And they never even learned why; was it better elsewhere, or worse? It could—or so he had decided from the utterances of the 6 P.M. radio— be that it consisted of both; it depended on the place.

And the world, now, was many places. The connectives had been destroyed. That which had made the once-castigated "uniformity."

" 'You understand,' " Father Handy chanted, singsong, from *Ruddigore*. And at once Tibor ceased drinking his coffee.

" 'I think I do,' " he wailed back, finishing the quotation. " 'That duty, duty must be done,' " he said, then. The coffee cup was set down, an elaborate rejection costing the use of many surge-gates opening and closing.

" 'The rule,' " Father Handy said, " 'applies to everyone.' "

Half to himself, with real bitterness, Tibor said, " 'To shirk the task.' " He turned his head, licked rapidly with his expert tongue, and gazed in deep, prolonged study at the priest. "What is it?"

It is, Father Handy thought, the fact that I am linked; I am part of a network that whips and quivers with the whole chain, shivered from above. And we believe—as you know—that the final motion is given from that Elsewhere that we receive the dim emanations out of, data which we strive honestly to understand and fulfill because we believe—we know—that what it wants is not only strong but correct.

"We're not slaves," he said aloud. "We are, after all, servants. We can quit; *you* can. Even I, if I felt it was right." But he would never; he had long ago decided, and taken a secret binding oath on it. "Who makes you do your job here?" he said, then.

Tibor said cautiously, "Well, you pay me."

"But I don't compel you."

"I have to eat. *That* does."

Father Handy said, "We know this: you can find many jobs, at any place; you could be anywhere working. Despite your—handicap."

"The Dresden Amen," Tibor said.

"Eh? What?" He did not understand.

"Sometime," Tibor said, "when you have the generator reconnected to the electronic organ, I'll play it for you; you'll recognize it. The Dresden Amen rises high. It points to an Above. Where you are bullied from."

"Oh no," Father Handy protested.

"Oh yes," Tibor said sardonically, and his pinched face withered with the abuse of his mis-emotion, his conviction. "Even if it's 'good,' a benign power. It still *makes* you do things. Just tell me this: Do I have to paint out anything I've already done? Or does this deal with the over-all mural?"

"With the final composition; what you've done is excellent. The color thirty-five-millimeter slides we sent on—they were delighted, those who looked at them; you know, the Church Eltern."

Reflecting, Tibor said, "Strange. You can still get color film and get it processed. But you can't get a daily newspaper."

"Well, there's the six-o'clock news on the radio," Father Handy pointed out. "From Salt Lake City." He waited hopefully. There was no answer; the limbless man drank the coffee silently. "Do you know," Father Handy said, "what the oldest word in the English language is?"

"No," Tibor said.

"'Might,'" Father Handy said. "In the sense of being mighty. It's *Macht* in the German. But it goes further back than Teutonic; it goes all the way back to the Hittites."

"Hmmm."

"The Hittite word *mekkis*. 'Power.'" Again he waited hopefully. "'Did you not chatter? Is this not woman's way?'" He was quoting from Mozart's *Magic Flute*. "'Man's way,'" he finished, "'is action.'"

Tibor said, "You're the one who's chattering."

"But you," Father Handy said, "must act. I had something to tell you." He reflected. "Oh yes. The sheep." He had, behind the church in a five-acre pasture, six ewes. "I got a ram late yesterday," he said, "from Theodore Benton. On loan, for breeding. Benton dumped him off while I was gone. He's an old ram; he has gray on his muzzle."

"Hmmm."

"A dog came and tried to run the flock, that red Irish-setter thing of the Yeats'. You know; it runs my ewes almost daily."

Interested now, the limbless man turned his head. "Did the ram—"

"Five times the dog approached the flock. Five times, moving very slowly, the ram walked toward the dog, leaving the flock behind. The dog, of course, stopped and stood still when he saw the ram coming toward him, and so the ram halted and pretended; he cropped." Father Handy smiled as he remembered. "How smart the old fellow was; I saw him crop, but he was watching the dog. The dog growled and barked, and the old fellow cropped on. And then again the dog moved in. But this time the dog ran, he bounded by the ram; he got between the ram and the flock."

"And the flock bolted."

"Yes. And the dog—you know how they do, learn to do—cut off one ewe, to run her down; they kill the ewe, then, or maim them, they get them from the belly." He was silent. "And the ram. He was too old; he couldn't run and catch up. He turned and watched."

Both men were then, together, silent.

"Can they think?" Tibor said. "The ram, I mean."

"I know," Father Handy said, "what I thought. I went to get my gun. To kill the dog. I had to."

"If it was me," Tibor said, "if I was that ram, and I saw that, I saw the dog get by me and run the flock and all I could do was watch—" He hesitated.

"You would wish," Father Handy said, "that you had already died."

"Yes."

"So death, as we teach the Servants of Wrath—we teach that it is a solution. Not an adversary, as the Christians taught, as Paul said. You remember their text. 'Death, where is thy sting? Grave, where is thy victory?' You see my point."

Tibor said slowly, "If you can't do your job, better to be dead. What is the job I have to do?"

In your mural, Father Handy thought, you must create His face.

"Him," he said. "And as He actually is."

After a puzzled pause Tibor said, "You mean His exact physical appearance?"

"Not," Father Handy said, "a subjective interpretation."

"You have photos? Vid data?"

"They've released a few to me. To be shown to you."

Staring at him, Tibor said, "You mean you have a *photo* of the Deus Irae?"

"I have a color photo in depth, what before the war they called 3-D. No animated pics, but this will be enough. I think."

"Let's see it." Tibor's tone was mixed, a compound of amazement and fear and the hostility of an artist hampered, impeded.

Passing into his inner office, Father Handy got the manila folder, came back with it, opened it, brought out the color 3-D photo of the God of Wrath, and held it forth. Tibor's right manual extensor seized it.

"That's the God," Father Handy said presently.

"Yes, you can see." Tibor nodded. "Those black eyebrows. That interwoven black hair; the eyes . . . I see pain, but he's smiling." His extensor abruptly returned the photo. "I can't paint him from that."

"Why not?" But Father Handy knew why not. The photo did not really catch the god-quality; it was the photo of a *man*. The god-quality; it could not be recorded by celluloid coated with a silver nitrate. "He was," he said, "at the time this photo was taken, having a luau in Hawaii. Eating young taro leaves with chicken and octopus. Enjoying himself. See the greed for the food, the lust creating an unnatural expression? He was relaxing on a Sunday afternoon before a speech before the faculty of some university; I forget which. Those happy days in the sixties."

"If I can't do my job," Tibor said, "its your fault."

" 'A poor workman always blames—' "

"You're not a box of tools." Both manual extensors slapped at the cart. "My tools are here. I don't blame; I use them. But you—you're my employer; you're telling me *what* to do, but how can I, from that one color shot? Tell me—"

"A Pilg. The Eltern of the Church say that if the photograph is inadequate—and it is, and we know it, all of us—then you must go on a Pilg until you find the Deus Irae, and they've sent documents pertaining to that."

Blinking in surprise, Tibor gaped, then protested, "But my metabattery! Suppose it gives out!"

Father Handy said, "So you do blame your tools." His voice was carefully controlled, quietly resounding.

At the stove, Ely said, "Fire him."

To her, Father Handy said, "I fire no one. A pun. Fire: their hell, the Christians. We don't have that," he reminded her. And then to Tibor he said the Great Verse of all the worlds, that which both men understood and yet did not grasp, could not, like Papagano with his net, entangle. He spoke it aloud as a bond holding them together in what *they,* the Christians, called *agape,* love. But this was higher than that; this was love and man and beautifulness, the three: a new trinity.

> Ich sih die liehte heide
> in gruner varwe stan.
> Dar süln wir alle gehen,
> die sumerzit enphahen.

After he said that, Tibor nodded, picked up his coffee cup once more, that difficult, elaborate motion and problem; sipped. The room became still and even Ely, the woman, did not chatter.

Outdoors, the cow which pulled Tibor's cart groaned huskily, shifted; perhaps, Father Handy thought, it is looking for, hoping for, food. It needs food for the body, we for our mind. Or everyone dies. We must have the mural; he must travel over a thousand miles, and if his cow dies or his battery gives out, then we expire with him; *he is not alone in this death.*

He wondered if Tibor knew that. If it would help to know. Probably not. So he did not say it; in this world nothing helped.

TWO

Neither man knew who had written the old poem, the medieval German words which could not be found in their Cassell's dictionary; they together, the two of them, had imagined out, summoned, found, the meaning of the words; they were certain they were right and understood. But not exactly. And Ely sneered.

But it was, I see the light-stricken thicket. In green—and then they did not quite know. It somehow stood in greenness. And we will all go there . . . was it *soon?* The summertime to—but to what? To reach? To find? Or was it—the summertime to leave?

They *felt* it, he and Tibor; a final truth, and yet it was, for them in their ignorance, without reference sources, both leaving and finding the summertime, the sun-struck woodland; it was life and the leaving of life fused, since they did not quite make it out rationally, and it frightened them, and yet they turned and returned to it, because—and perhaps exactly because they could not understand—it was a balm; it salved them.

Now, Father Handy and Tibor needed a power—mekkis, Father Handy thought to himself—to come from Above and aid them . . . on this, the Servants of Wrath agreed with the Christians: the good power lay Above, *Ubrem Sternenzelt,* as Schiller had once said: above the band of stars. Yes, *beyond* the stars; this they were clear on; this was modern German.

But it was strange, depending on a poem whose meaning one did not actually grasp; he wondered, as he unfolded and searched through the old stained gasstation maps once given out free in prewar days, if this was not a stigma of degeneracy. An omen of badness . . . not just that times were bad but that they themselves had become bad; the quality was lodged within them.

His conference now was with the Dominus McComas, his superior in the hierarchy of the Servants of Wrath; the Dominus sat, large and tepid, with strangely cruel teeth, as if he tore things, not necessarily living, in fact much harder—as if he did a job, a profession, teethwise.

"Carl Lufteufel," the Dominus McComas said, "was a son of a bitch. As a man." He added that because of course one did not speak of the god part of the godman, the Deus Irae, like that. "And," he said, "I'll give you ten to five that he made martinis with *sweet* vermouth."

"Did you ever drink sweet vermouth straight or with ice?" Father Handy asked.

"It's sweet piss," McComas grated in his horrid, low voice, and, as he spoke, cut into his spongy gum with the tail of a wooden match. "I am not kidding; it's nothing but horse piss they've bought."

"Diabetic horses," Father Handy said.

"Yeah, passing sugar." McComas grunted a ha-ha; his round, red—red as if they had short-circuited and the metal in them had heated up, dangerous and improper—eyes sparked; but this was normal, as was his halfzipped fly. "So your inc," McComas grated, "is going to roll all the way to Los Angeles. Is it downhill?" And this time he laughed so that he spat onto the table. Ely, seated off in a corner, knitting, stared at him with such flat hate that Father Handy felt uncomfortable and turned his attention to the creased gas-station maps.

"Carleton Lufteufel," Father Handy said, "was Chairman of the Energy Research and Development Administration from 1982 to the beginning of the war." He spoke half to himself. "To the use of the gob." The great objectless bomb, a bomb which detonated not at one particular spot on the Earth's surface but which acted so as to contaminate a layer of the atmosphere itself. It therefore (and this was the sort of weapons-theorizing that had gone on prior to World War Three) could not be headed off, as a missile could be by an antimissile, or a manned bomber, no matter how fast—and they had gone quite fast, by 1982—by, incredibly, a biplane. A slow biplane.

In 1978 the biplane had reappeared in the D-III. Defensive III, a flap-flap man-made pelican which held within it a limitless fuel supply; it could circle, at low altitude, for months, while, within, the pilot lived off his suit as Our Grandparents had lived off trees and shrubs. The D-III biplane had a tropic device which directed its efforts when a manned bomber, even at fantastic altitude, came; the D-III began to ascend when the bomber was still a thousand miles away, releasing from between its wings a sinkerlike weight of vast density which pulled the plane to the proper altitude; the D-III and its pilot were actually jerked high, where no atmosphere to speak of existed. And the sinker—it had actually been called that even though it did just the opposite; it in fact lifted—carried the biplane and the man within toward the manned bomber, and all at once the two objects met. And everyone died. But "everyone" was only three men in all: two in the bomber, one in the D-III. And, below, a city lived on, lit up, composedly functioning.

While other D-IIIs circled, circled, month after

month; like certain raptors, they hovered for a seeming eternity.

However, it was not truly eternity. The antimissiles and the D-IIIs had kept off the fatal wasps for a finite time, and then at last the Dies Irae had come—for everyone, because of the gob, the great objectless device which Carleton Lufteufel had detonated from a satellite at an apogee of five thousand miles. It had been imagined that the U.S. would in some mysterious fashion survive and prosper, perhaps because of a New Year's Eve funny-hat artifact distributed to the multimillions of patriotic USers; it connected to cephalic veins and gave restitution to a bloodstream rapidly losing red corpuscles. The vacuum-cleaner salesmen's convention-style headgear, however, had been finite, too; it had failed for many people long before the Krankheit—the sickness—had faded. The great, grand corporation which had sold the Pentagon and the White House on the funny hats—it too had disappeared, gotten not by bone-marrow-destroying fallout but by direct hits from missiles which ducked and wove faster than the anti-ms twisted and darted. Don't look back, Satchel Paige had once said; something may be gaining on you. The missiles from People's China had not looked back and the things gaining on them had not reached them in time; China could die with the happy knowledge that out of their miserable underground "backyard" factories they had developed a weapon which even Dr. Porsche, had he still been alive, would have shaken his head at— nodded at with admiration.

But what, Doctor, Father Handy thought to himself as he shuffled and unfolded the ancient gas-station maps, had been the authentic really dirty weapon of the war? The gob of the Deus Irae had killed the most people . . . probably about a billion. No, the gob of Carleton Lufteufel, now worshiped as the God of Wrath—

that had not been it, unless one went by mere numbers.

No; he had his own favorite, and, although it had killed only a relatively few million people, it impressed him: its evil was so blatant; it glowed and stank, as a U.S. Congressman had once said, like a dead mackerel in the night's dark. And it, like the gob, was a U.S. weapon.

It was a nerve gas.

It caused the organs of the body to eat one another.

"Well," the Dominus McComas growled, picking at his hardy teeth, "if the inc can do it, fine. If I was an Elter I wouldn't give a damn if it looked like Lufteufel or not; I'd just get a good fat wicked bloated pig-face up there; you know, a swilling face." And his own swilling face beamed, and how strange it was, Father Handy thought, because McComas looked like one would *imagine* the Deus Irae to look . . . and yet, the color photo had shown a man with pain-smeared eyes, a man who seemed ill in a deep and dreadful way even as he gorged on roast chicken with a lei around his neck and a girl—not pretty—to his right . . . a man with shiny, heavy, tumbled black hair and too much stubble, even though no doubt he carefully shaved; it was subdermal, showing through: not his fault, and yet it was *the mark*. But of what? Blackness was not evil; blackness was what Martin Luther in his translation of Genesis had meant when he said, *"Und die Erde war ohne Form und leer." Leer;* that was it. That was what blackness was; when spoken it sounded like "layer" . . . a film negative, which, having been exposed to unshielded light, had, due to chemical action, turned to absolute opaqueness, to this quality of *leer*ness, this layer of glaucomalike blindness. It was like Oedipus wandering; what he saw, or rather what he failed to see. His eyes were not destroyed; they were really covered: it was a membrane. And so he, Father Handy, did not hate Carle-

ton Lufteufel, because that billion who had died had
not gone like those who had been gassed by the U.S.
nerve gas; its death had not been monstrous.

And yet this had ended the war; there was, after the
toxic rain had ended, insufficient personnel to continue.
De mortuis nil nisi bonum, he thought: Of the dead
only say good things, such as—well, he thought, perhaps this: You died because of the idiots whom you
hired to rule you and protect you and collect terrible
taxes from you. Therefore, who was the ultimate cretin,
you or they? Anyhow, both had perished. The Pentagon
had long ago gone; the White House, the VIP shelters
. . . *de mortuis nil nisi malum,* he thought, correcting
the old saying to make it come out the more wisely: Of
the dead only speak evil. Because they were that stupid;
it was cretinism carried to the dimension of the satanic.

—Carried to the point of supinely reading the 'papes
and watching the TV and doing nothing when Carleton
Lufteufel had given his speech in 1983 at Cheyenne, the
so-called Numerical Fallacy speech in which he had
made the inspired, brilliant point, much head-nodded
at, that it was not so that a nation needed a certain
number of survivors to function; a nation, Lufteufel had
explained, does not reside in its people at all but in its
know-how. As long as the data-repositories are safe, the
time capsules of micropools buried miles under—if they
remained, then (as he had phrased it, equal, many in
Washington said, to the "blood-sweat-tears" speech of
Churchill's, decades before) "our patriotic idiosyncratic
ethnic patterns survive because they can be learned by
any replacement generation."

The replacement generation, however, had not had
the wherewithal to dig up the data-repositories, because they had a more important task, one overlooked
by Lufteufel: that of growing food to keep themselves
alive. The same problems which had lashed the Pil-

grims, those of clearing land, planting, protecting crops and livestock. Pigs, cows, and sheep, corn and wheat, beets and carrots: those became the vital patriotic idiosyncratic ethnic preoccupations, not the aural text of some great American epic poetic stupidity such as Whittier's *Snowbound*.

"I say," McComas rumbled, "don't send your inc; don't have him do the mural at all; get a Complete. He'll roll along on that cow-cart for a hundred or so miles and then he'll come to a place where there's no road, and he'll go into a ditch and that'll be that. It's no favor to him, Handy. It just means you're killing some poor limbless fart who admittedly paints well—"

"Paints," Father Handy said, "better than any artist that SOW knows of." He pronounced the initials as a word, as "sow"—the female pig—so as to plague McComas, who insisted it always be spoken as three initials or at least as "sow" to rhyme with "mow."

McComas's short-circuited red eyes focused malignly on him, and he searched for a cutting, tearing, oral return remark; while he did so, Ely said all at once, "Here comes Miss Rae."

"Oh," Father Handy said, and blinked. Because it was Lurine Rae who made into fact the dots, jots, and tittles of Servants of Wrath dogma; at least as far as he personally was concerned.

Here she came now, red-haired and so small-boned that he always imagined that she could fly . . . the idea of witches entered his mind when he saw Lurine Rae unexpectedly, because of this lightness. She rode horseback constantly, and this was the "real" reason for her springiness—but it was not merely the lithe motion of an athletic woman; nor was it ethereal either. Hollow-boned, he had decided, like a bird. And that connected once more in his mind women and birds; hence once more Papagano, the birdcatcher's, song: He would make a net for birds and then he would make, someday, a net for a little wife or a little lady who would sleep by his side, and Father Handy, seeing Lurine, felt the wicked old ram-animal within him awake; the evil of substantiality itself manifested its insidious being at the heart of his nature.

Distressing. But he was used to it; in fact he enjoyed it—enjoyed, really, her.

"Morning," Lurine said to him, then saw the Dominus McComas, whom she did not like; she wrinkled her nose and her freckles writhed: all the pale red, that of her hair, her skin, her lips, all twisted in aversion, and she, too, bared her teeth, back at him. Only her teeth were tiny and regular, and made not to grind—as for instance the prehistoric uncooked seeds—but to neatly sever.

Lurine had *biting* teeth. Not the massive chewing kind.

She, he knew, nipped. Knew? Guessed, rather. Because he had not really ever come near her; he kept a distance between them.

The ideology of the Servants of Wrath connected with the Augustinian view of women; there was fear involved, and then of course the dogma got entangled with the old cult of Mani, the Albigensian Heresy of Provinçal France, the Catharists. To them, flesh and the world had been evil; they had abstained. But their poets and knights had worshiped women, had deified them; the *domina*, so enticing, so vital . . . even the mad ones, the *dominae* of Carcassonne who had carried their dead lovers' hearts in small jeweled boxes. And the—was it merely insane, or rather more perverted?— Catharist knights who had actually carried in enameled boxes their mistresses' dried dung . . . it had been a cult ruthlessly wiped out by Innocent III, and perhaps rightly so. But—

For all its excesses, the Albigensian knight-poets had known the worth of women; she was not man's servant and not even merely his "weak rib," the side of him who had been so readily tempted. She was—well, a good question; as he got a chair for Lurine and poured her coffee, he thought: Some supreme value lies in this slight, freckled, pale, red-haired, horse-riding girl of twenty. Supreme as is the mekkis of the God of Wrath Himself. But not a mekkis; not Macht, not power or might. It is more a—mystery. Hence, gnostic wisdom is involved, knowledge hidden behind a wall so fragile, so entrancing . . . but undoubtedly a fatal knowledge. Interesting, that truth could be a terminal possession. The woman knew the truth, lived with it, yet it did not kill her. But when she uttered it—he thought of Cassandra and of the female Oracle at Delphi. And felt afraid.

Once he had said to Lurine, in the evening after a few drinks, "You carry what Paul called the *sting*."

"The sting of death," Lurine had promptly recalled, "is sin."

"Yes." He had nodded. And she bore it, and it no more killed her than the viper's poison killed it . . . or the H-warhead missiles menaced themselves. A knife, a sword, had two ends: one a handle, the other a blade; the gnosis of this woman was for her gripped by the safe end, the handle; but when she extended it—he saw, flashing, the light of the slight blade.

But what, for the Servants of Wrath, did sin consist of? The weapons of the war; one naturally thought of the psychotic and psychopathic cretins in high places in dead corporations and government agencies, now dead as individuals; the men at drafting boards, the idea men, the planners, the policy boys and P.R. infants—like grass, their flesh. Certainly that had been sin, what they had done, but that had been without knowledge. Christ, the God of the Old Sect, had said that about His murderers: they did not know what they were up to. Not knowledge *but the lack of knowledge* had made them into what they had been, frozen into history as they gambled for His garments or stuck His side with the spear. There was knowledge in the Christian Bible, in three places that he personally knew of—despite the rule within the Servants of Wrath hierarchy against reading the Christian sacred texts. One part lay in the Book of Job. One in Ecclesiastes. The last, the final note, had been Paul's letters to the Corinthians, and then it had ended, and Tertullian and Origen and Augustine and Thomas Aquinas—even the divine Abelard; none had added an iota in two thousand years.

And now, he thought, *we know.* The Catharists had come bleakly close, had guessed one piece: that the world lay in the control of an evil adversary and not the good god. What they had not guessed was contained in Job, that the "good god" was a god of wrath—was in fact evil.

"Like Shakespeare has Hamlet say to Ophelia," McComas growled at Lurine. " 'Get thee to a nunnery.' "

Lurine, sipping coffee, said prettily, "Up yours."

"See?" the Dominus McComas said to Father Handy.

"I see," he said carefully, "that you can't order people to be this or that; they have what used to be called an ontological nature."

Scowling, McComas said, "Whazzat?"

"Their intrinsic nature," Lurine said sweetly. "What they *are.* You ignorant rustic religious cranks." To Father Handy she said, "I finally made up my mind. "I'm joining the Christian Church."

Hoarsely guffawing, McComas shook, belly-wise, not Santa Claus belly but belly of hard, grinding animal. "*Is* there a Christian Church anymore? In this area?"

Lurine said, "They're very gentle and kind, there."

"They have to be," McComas said. "They have to plead to get people to come in. We don't need to plead; they come to us for protection. From Him." He jerked his thumb upward. At the God of Wrath, not in his man-form, not as he had appeared on Earth as Carleton Lufteufel, but as the mekkis-spirit everywhere. Above, here, and ultimately below; in the grave, to which they all were dragged at last.

The final enemy which Paul had recognized—death—had had its victory after all; Paul had died for nothing.

And yet here sat Lurine Rae, sipping coffee, announcing calmly that she intended to join a discredited, withering, elderly sect. The husk of the former world, which had shown its chiltinous shell, its wickedness; for it had been *Christians* who had designed the ter-weps, the terror weapons.

The descendants of those who had sung square-wrought, pious Lutheran hymns had designed, at German cartels, the evil instruments which had shown up the "God" of the Christian Church for what he was.

Death was not an antagonist, the last enemy, as Paul had thought; death was the release from bondage to the God of Life, the Deus Irae. In death one was free from Him—and only in death.

It was the God of Life who was the evil god. And in fact the only God. And Earth, this world, was the only kingdom. And they, all of them; they constituted his servants, in that they carried out, had always done so, over the thousands of years, his commands. And his reward had been in keeping both with his nature and with his commands: it had been the Ira. The Wrath.

And yet here sat Lurine. So it made no sense.

* * *

Later, when the Dominus McComas had ambled, trudged off on foot to see about his business, Father Handy sat with Lurine.

"Why?" he said.

Shrugging, Lurine said, "I like kindly people. I like Dr. Abernathy."

He stared at her. Jim Abernathy, the local Christian priest in Charlottesville; he detested the man—if Abernathy was really a man; he seemed more a castrato, fit, as put in *Tom Jones*, for entry in the gelding races. "He gives you exactly what?" he demanded. "Self-help. The 'think pleasant thoughts and all will be—' "

"No," Lurine said.

Ely said dryly, "She's sleeping with that acolyte. That Pete Sands. You know; the bald young man with acne."

"Ringworm," Lurine corrected.

"At least," Ely said, "get him a fungicide oinment to rub on his scalp. So you don't catch it."

"Mercury," Father Handy said. "From a peddler, itinerant; you can buy for about five U.S. silver half-dollars—"

"Okay!" Lurine said angrily.

"See?" Ely said to her husband.

He saw; it was true and he knew it.

"So he's not a *gesunt*," Lurine said. Gesunt—a healthy person. Not made sick or maimed by the war, as the incompletes had been. Pete Sands was a kranker, a sick one; it showed on his marred head, hairless, his pocked and pitted face. Back to the Anglo-Saxon peasant with his pox, he thought with surprising venom. Was it jealousy? He amazed himself.

Nodding toward Father Handy, Ely said, speaking to Lurine, "Why not sleep with him? He's a gesunt."

"Aw, come on," Lurine said in her small, quiet, but deadly boiling-hot angry voice; when she became really terribly furious her entire face flushed, and she sat as stiffly as if calcified.

"I mean it," Ely said, in a sort of loud, high screech.

"Please," Father Handy said, trying to calm his wife.

"But why come here?" Ely asked Lurine. "To announce you're going to revert, is that it? Who cares? Revert. In fact, sleep with Abernathy; a lot of good it'll do you." She made it meaningful; she put over the significance of her words by the wild tone alone. Women had such great ability at that; they possessed such a range. Men, in contrast, grunted, as with McComas; they resorted, as in his case, to an ugly chuckle. That was little enough.

Trying to sound wise, Father Handy said to Lurine, "Have you thought it over carefully? There's a stigma attached; after all, you do live by sewing and weaving and spinning—you depend on goodwill in this community, and if you join Abernathy's church—"

"Freedom of conscience," Lurine said.

"Oh god," Ely moaned.

"Listen," Father Handy said. Reaching out, he took hold of both of Lurine's hands, held them with his own. He explained, then, patiently. "Just because you're sleeping with Sands, that doesn't force you to accept their religious teachings. 'Freedom of conscience' also means freedom *not* to accept dogma; do you see? Now look, dear." She was twenty; he was forty-two, and felt sixty; he felt, holding her hands, like a tottering old ram, some defanged creature mumbling and drooling, and he cringed at his self-image. But he continued anyhow. "They believed for two thousand years in a good god. And now we know it's not true. There is a god, but he is—you know as well as I do; you were a kid during the war, but you remember and you can see; you've seen the miles of dust that once were bodies . . . I don't understand how you can in all honesty, intellectually or morally, accept an ideology that teaches that *good* played a decisive role in what happened. See?"

She did not disengage her hands. But she remained inert, so passive that he felt as if he held deceased organisms; the physical sensation repelled him and he voluntarily released her. She then picked up her coffee cup once more, with tranquility. And she said, "All right; we know that a Carleton Lufteufel, Chairman of the ERDA of the United States Government, existed. But he was a man. Not a god."

"A man in form," Father Handy said, "made by God. In God's image, according to your own sacred writ."

She became silent; this she could not answer.

"Dear," Father Handy said, "to believe in the Old Church is to flee. To try to escape the present. We, *our* church; we try to live in this world and face what's happening and how we stand. We're honest. We, as living creatures, are in the hands of a merciless and angry deity and will be until death wipes us from the slate of his records. If perhaps one could believe in a god of death . . . but unfortunately—"

"Maybe there is one," Lurine said abruptly.

"Pluto?" He laughed.

"Maybe God releases us from our torment," she answered steadily. "And I may find him in Abernathy's church. Anyhow—" She glanced up, flushed and small and determined and lovely. "I won't worship a psychotic ex-official of the U.S. ERDA as a deity; that's not being realistic; that's—" She gestured. "It's wrong," she said, as if speaking to herself, trying to convince herself.

"But," Father Handy said, "he lives."

She stared at him, sadly, and very troubled.

"We," he continued, "as you know, are painting him. And we are sending our inc, our artist, to seek him out;

we have Richfield Station and AAA maps . . . call it
pragmatism, if you want; Abernathy once said that to
me. But what does *he* worship? Not anything. You show
me. *Show me*." He slammed his flat hand on the table,
savagely.

"Well," Lurine said, "maybe this is—"

"The prelude? To the real life to come? Do you gen-
uinely believe that? Listen, dear; St. Paul believed that
Christ would return in his own lifetime. That the 'New
Kingdom' would begin in the first century A.D. *Did it?*"

"No," she said.

"And everything that Paul wrote or thought is based
on that fallacy. But we base our beliefs on no fallacy;
we know that Carleton Lufteufel served as the manifestation on Earth of the Deity, and he showed his true
character, and it was wrathful. You can *see* it in every
handful of dirt and rubble. You've seen it for sixteen
years. If there were any psychiatrists alive they'd tell
you the truth, what you're trying to do. It's called—a
fugue." He became silent, then.

Ely added, "And she gets to sleep with Sands."

No one said anything to that; it, too, consisted of a
fact. And a fact was a thing, and words could not retort
to a thing: it required another and greater thing. And
Lurine Rae, and the Old Church, did not have that; it
possessed only nice words like "agape" and "caritas"
and "mercy" and "salvation."

"When you have lived through the ter-weps," Father
Handy said to Lurine, "and the gob, you no longer can
live by words alone. See?"

Lurine nodded, troubled and confused and unhappy.

THREE

During the war many toxic drugs had been developed, and afterward, these drugs—a vast variety of kinds—lay about amid the general chaos and could be found here and there like everything else. And Peter Sands took particular interest in these drugs, because some—a few, anyhow—of them, although developed originally as weapons against the enemy, to impede, disorient, and altogether befuddle his faculties, had a certain positive value.

At least so he believed. If one was careful, one could concoct a potion, several drugs taken in conjunction; one became disoriented, but a certain expansion or heightened lucidity also occurred. Green little methamphets, shiny red 'zines, white flat discs of code segmented sometimes into halves, sometimes when stronger into four parts, tiny yellow elves . . . he had gathered an inventory which he carefully kept hidden. No one but himself knew of this trove which he hoarded . . . and, while collecting and hoarding, he experimented.

He believed that the so-called hallucinations caused by some of these drugs (with emphasis, he continually reminded himself, on the word "some") were not hallucinations at all, but perceptions of other zones of reality. Some of them were frightening; some appeared lovely.

Oddly, he poked and tinkered with the former; per-

haps a long Puritan background had made him—he
conjectured—masochistic; anyhow, it was into the
realm of terror that he liked to venture very slightly . . .
he did not wish either to go too far or to stay too long,
but he wished for a fair glimpse.

It reminded him of his dad, who, one day before the
war at an amusement park, had tried out a shock machine; you put in a dime, seized two handles, and grad-
ually moved them apart. The farther apart, the greater
the electric current; one learned just how much he could
stand, how far apart he could bear to pry the two handles. Watching his sweating, red-faced father, Peter
Sands had felt admiration, had seen his dad's grip on
the handles become tighter, more vigorous, the greater
the gap became. And yet it was obviously a powerful—
too powerful, ultimately—antagonist which his father
strove against; finally his father had, with a grunt of
pain, let go entirely.

But how admirable his dad had been, and of course
he was showing off to Pete, who, at eight years old,
thought his dad was great indeed. Himself, he had for
one fraction of a second touched the handles—and
leaped away in fright; he could not endure an instant of
the shock. He was, indeed, not like his dad . . . at
least in his own estimation.

So now he had his leftover ter-wep pills. Which he
mixed, alchemist-wise, in proportions of a guarded variety and quantity. And always he made sure that another
person was present, so that a standard phenothiazine
could be given orally, if he passed too far in, out, down,
whatever direction the drugs carried one.

"I'm nuts," he had said to Lurine Rae, once, in can-
did admission. And yet he kept on; he inspected the offerings of each peddler who passed through Charlottesville . . . inspected and often bought. He owned vast
pharmacopoeias and could tell, usually at a glance,

what a given pill, tablet, or spansule consisted of, no matter how arcane; he recognized the hallmark of every prewar ethical house: in this his wisdom was complete.

"Then," Lurine had said, "stop."

But he didn't want to, because he was seeking something. Not just diddling himself but searching—the goal was there, but obscured by a membrane; and he strove, via the medication, to lift the membrane, the curtain—this was how he depicted it to himself, a rationalization, perhaps, but why else do this? Because often he did suffer fear and disorientation, sometimes depression and even, but rarely, murderous polymorphic rage.

Punishment? No, he had often thought and replied. He did not seek to injure himself, to impair his faculties, to develop liver or kidney toxicity; he read brochures, carefully watched for side effects . . . and certainly he did not want to turn berserk and injure another; pale, pretty Lurine, for example. But—

"We can see Carleton Lufteufel with our unaided senses," he explained to Lurine. "But I believe—" There was another order of reality and the unaided eyes did not penetrate this; if you took ultraviolet and infrared rays as an example . . .

Lurine, curled up in a chair opposite him, smoking an Algerian briar pipe with a prewar utterly dried-out Dutch cavendish mixture in it, said, "Instead of taking pills, build instruments that register its presence. Whatever it is you're after. Read it off a dial. That's safer." Always she was afraid that he would enter a drug-induced state and not return; after all, the medications were not medications: they were neurological and metabolic enzymes, poorly understood even by their makers . . . their effects varied from person to person.

"I don't want to see a reading on a dial," he answered. "It's not a record I want; it's an—" He gestured. "An experience."

Lurine sighed. "Let it come to you, then. Sit and wait."

"I can't wait," he said. "Because it won't come this side of the grave." That enemy which the New Church, the SOWs, craved: their solution. Although at the same time the SOWers liked to think of themselves, the survivors of the war, as the Chosen, the elite whom the God of Wrath had spared.

He saw in their logic the basic fault. If the God of Wrath was evil, as the SOWers maintained, *he would spare not the good but the most evil.* Hence, by their own logic, they were the wicked of the world; like Carleton Lufteufel himself, they were alive because they were too wicked to be offered the healing balm of death.

Such lunatic logic bored him. So he turned back to the display of pills on the table before him, in his little living room.

"Okay," Lurine said. "What *is* there that you're seeking? You must have some idea, at least as to its worth . . . or you wouldn't be always buying those little placebos for all that silver the peddlers charge. I'm very unhappy; maybe tonight I'll join you." Today she had told Father Handy that she intended to join the Christian Church, but she had not told either Pete Sands or Dr. Abernathy. As usual, she was having it both ways . . . an instinct kept her from making the terminal move.

Pete, his forehead wrinkling, said slowly, "I saw once what's called *der Todesstachel.* At least that's what your buddy Father Handy and that inc Tibor would call it; they like those German theological terms."

"What's *ein Todesstachel?*" she asked. She had never heard the word before, but she knew that *Tod* meant death.

Pete said somberly, "The sting of death. But listen.

'Sting,' as when a bug or a nettle stings you . . . that's the *modern* usage. It now means being touched by a poison-filled stinger, as with a bee. But it didn't always mean that. In the old days, as for example when the King James scholars wrote the phrase 'Death, where is thy sting?' they meant it in the old sense. Which is—" He hesitated. "Like being stung by a remark. Do you get it? Stung, for instance, into rage, hurt by a remark. It meant to be pierced by a dartlike point. In dueling, for instance, they stung each other; we would say 'pricked,' now. So Paul didn't mean that death stung the way a scorpion stings, with a tail and a sac of poison, an irritant; he meant a *piercing*." Paul had meant what he himself, Pete Sands, had once, under the influence of drugs, experienced.

He had been fighting; the drugs had set off a polymorphic, circus-movement destructiveness and he had strode about smashing things, and, since it was Lurine's small apartment, he had smashed her possessions and then, incredibly, had, when she tried to stop him, kicked and hit her. And when he did so, he felt the sting—the sting in its older sense: the deep piercing of his body by a sharp-pointed metal gaff, a barbed spear such as fishermen use to secure heavy fish, once netted.

In all his life he had never experienced anything so real. He had, as the gaff entered his side, doubled up in utter pain, and Lurine, who had been ducking and dodging, had halted at once in concern for him.

The gaff—the metal barbed hook itself—came at the bottom end of a long pole, a spear, which ascended from Earth to heaven, and he had, in that awful instant as he rolled doubled up in agony, glimpsed the Persons at the top end of the spear, those who held the pole that bridged the two worlds. Three figures with warm but impassive eyes. They had not twisted the gaff within him; They had simply held it there until, in his pain, he

had begun by slow and gradual degrees to become
awake. That was the purpose of this sting: to wake him
from his sleep, the sleep of all mankind, from which
everyone would one day, in the twinkling of an eye, as
Paul had said, be roused. "Behold," Paul had said, "I
tell you a mystery. We shall not all sleep but shall be
changed, in the twinkling of an eye." But oh, the pain.
Did it take this much to awaken him? Must everyone
suffer like this? Would the gaff pierce him again sometime? He dreaded it, and yet he recognized that the
three figures, the Trinity, were right; this had to be
done; he had to be roused. And yet—

He now got out a book, opened it, and read aloud to
Lurine, who liked to be read to if it wasn't too long and
declamatory. He read a small, simple poem, without
telling her the author.

> Mother, I cannot mind my wheel;
> My fingers ache, my lips are dry;
> Oh! if you felt the pain I feel!
> But oh, who ever felt as I!

Closing the book, he asked, "What do you think of
that?"

" 'Sokay."

He said, "Sappho. Translated by Landor. Probably
from one word, from a 'fragment.' But it reminds one of
Gretchen am Spinnrade—in the first part of Goethe's
Faust." And he thought, *Meine Ruh ist hin. Mein
Herz ist schwer.* My peace is gone, my heart is heavy.
Amazing, so much alike. Did Goethe know? The Sap-
pho poem was better, being shorter. And it, at least as
done by Landor, was in English, and he, unlike the
SOWer Father Handy, did not delight in strange
tongues; in fact he dreaded them. Too many ter-weps

had come for example from Germany; he could not forget that.

"Who was Sappho?" Lurine asked.

Presently he said, "The finest poet the world ever knew. Even in fragments. You can have Pindar; he was third-rate." Again he inspected the display of pills; what to take, what combination? To strive by means of these to reach that other land which he knew existed, beyond the gate of death perhaps.

"Tell me," Lurine said, smoking away on her cheap Algerian briar pipe—it was all she had been able to purchase from a peddler; the U.K. rose briars were too dear—and watching him acutely, "What it was like that time you took those methamphetamines and saw the Devil."

He laughed.

"What's funny?"

"It sounds like," he said, "you know. Forked tail, cloven hoof, horns."

But she was serious. "It wasn't. Tell me again."

He did not like to remember his vision of the Antagonist, what Martin Luther had called "our ancient foe on earth." So he got a glass of water, carefully selected several assorted pills, and swallowed them.

"Horizontal eyes," Lurine said. "You told me that. And without pupils. Just slots."

"Yes." He nodded.

"And he was above the horizon. And unmoving. He'd always been there, you said. Was he blind?"

"No. He perceived *me,* for instance. In fact all of us, all life. He waits." They are wrong, the Servants of Wrath, Pete thought; upon death we can be delivered over to the Antagonist: it will—may—not be a release at all, only the start. "You see," he said, "he was so placed that he viewed straight across the surface of the world, as if the world were flat and his gaze, like a laser beam, traveled on without end, forever. It had no focus point, such as a lens creates."

"What did you take just now?"

"Narkazine."

"Nark has to do with sleep. Zine is a stimulant, though. Does it stimulate you to sleep?"

"It dulls the frontal lobe and permits the thalamus free activity. So—" He quickly swallowed two tiny gray pills. "I take these to hold back the thalamus." Brain metabolism, the vasodilation and -constriction, was his hobby; he knew the map of the human brain and what a little-too-slight supply of blood to this or that portion could do—that it could forever turn a kindly, warm, perceptive man into a narrow, rigid, suspicious, brooding quasi-paranoid. So he was so careful; he wanted primarily to affect the hormonal secretions of his adrenal-class glands without too much vasoconstriction. And the amphetamines were vasoconstrictors and hence dangerous; they could permanently damage the personality on a physiological basis.

All this the great ethical houses had discovered and duly made available, ter-wep-wise, to the Pentagon in the '60s and '70s—and had seen used in the '80s.

But on the other hand, the methamphetamines inhibited the secretion of adrenalin, and this, for some personalities, was vital; schizophrenia had at last, like cancer, been unmasked; cancer consisted of a virus and schizophrenia had turned out to be an overproduction of serotonin which the brain could not handle; hence the hallucinations—true hallucinations, although the dividing line between hallucination and authentic vision had become thin indeed.

"I don't understand you," Lurine said. "You take those goddamn pills and then you see something just awful—Satan himself. Or that hook you talk about, that gaff that penetrated your side. And yet you go back. And you're not just bored; it's not that." Puzzled, she regarded him.

Pete said, "I have to know. That's all. To experience, to know, is to *be*. I want to be."

"You are," she pointed out, practically.

"Listen," Pete said. "God—the authentic God, He of the Bible, Whom we worship, not that Carleton Lufteufel—is searching for us; the Bible is a chronicle of God's search for man. Not man's search for God. Do you understand? And I want to go as far toward Him, to meet Him, as I can."

"How did man and God get separated?" Like a child, she listened attentively, awaiting the true tale.

Pete said cryptically, "A quarrel so old that the story is garbled. Somehow God set man up where He could reach man daily, regularly; they were in direct touch, the way you and I are now. But something happened and somehow they wound up like Leibnitz's windowless monads, near each other but unable to perceive anything outside; only able to scrutinize their own beings. A sort of schizophrenia evidently set in, on the part of one of them or both; autism—separation. And then man—"

"Man was driven out. Physically away."

Pete said, "Evidently man did something, or anyhow God thought he had. We don't know precisely what it was. He was corrupted, anyhow, through nature or some natural substance; something made by God and part of His creation. So man sank out of direct contact and down to the level of mere creation. And we have to make our way back."

"And you do it through those pills."

He said, simply, "It's all I know. I don't have *natural* visions. I want to take the journey back until I stand face to face with Him as man once did—did, and elected not to. Beyond doubt, some thing or some *one* tempted him away and into doing something else. *Man voluntarily gave up that relationship because he thought he had found something better."* Half to himself he added, "So we wound up with Carleton Lufteufel and the gob and the ter-weps."

"I like the idea of being tempted," Lurine said; she relit her pipe, it having gone out. "Everyone does. Those pills tempt you; you're still doing it. Men— people like you—have prairie-dog blood; they're in- sanely curious. Make a funny noise and out you pop from your burrow to witness whatever's taking place. Just in case." She pondered. "A wonder. That's what you crave and he—the first of us in the Garden— craved. What before the war they called a 'spectacular.' It's the big tent syndrome." She smiled. "And I'll tell you something else. You know why you want to be at ringside? So you can be with *them."*

"Who?"

"The big boys. Hubris. Vainglory. Man saw God and he said to himself, Gee whiz, how come He gets to be God and I'm stuck with—"

"And I'm doing this now."

Lurine said, "Learn to be what Christ called 'meek.' I bet you don't know what that means. Remember those supermarkets before the war; when someone pushed a cart into line ahead of you, and you accepted it—that's your faulty idea of 'meek.' Actually meek means 'tamed,' as in a tamed animal."

Startled, he said, "Really?"

"Then it got to mean humble, or even merciful, or long-suffering, or even bad things like weak and soft. But originally it meant to lose the quality of violence. In the Bible it means specifically to be free from resent- ment regarding injuries done to you." She laughed with delight. "You stupid fool," she said, then. "You prattle but you don't know a thing, really."

He said stiffly, "Hanging around that pedant Father Handy has hardly made you meek. In any of the senses of the word."

At that, Lurine laughed until she choked. "Oh god." She breathed. "We can have a ferocious argument, now: Which of us is the meeker? Hell, I'm a *lot* meeker than you!" She rocked with amusement.

He ignored her. Because of the stew of pills which he had taken; they had begun to work on him.

He saw a figure, suddenly, with laughing eyes, whom he supposed to be Jesus. It had to be. The man, with white-thatched hair, wore a toga and Greek greaves. He was young, with brawny shoulders, and he grinned in a gentle, happy way as he stood clutching to his chest an enormous and heavy clasp-bound book. Except for the classic greaves, he might—from the wild cut of his hair—have been Saxon.

Jesus Christ! Pete thought.

The white-haired brawny youth—my god, he was built like a blacksmith!—unbuckled the book and opened it to display two wide pages. Pete saw writing in a foreign language, held forward for him to read:

KAI THEOS EIN HO LOGOS

Pete couldn't make it out, nor the jumble of other words which, although neatly inscribed, swam before him in this vision, snatches meaningless to him, such as *koimeitheisometha . . . keoiesis . . . titheimi . . .* he just could not even tell if it was a genuine language or not: communication or the nonsense phantoms of a dream.

The flaxen-haired youth shut the great book which he held and then, abruptly, was gone. It was like, his coming and going, an old wartime laser hologram, but without sound.

"You shouldn't listen to that anyhow," a voice said within Pete's head, as if his own thought processes had passed from his control. "All that mumbo-jumbo was to impress you. Did he tell you his name, that man? No, he did not."

Turning, Pete made out the bobbing, floating image of a small clay pot, a modest object, fired but without glaze; merely hardened. A utilitarian object, from the soil of the ground. It was lecturing him against being awed—which he had been—and he appreciated it.

"I'll tell you my name," the pot said. "I'm Oh Ho."

To himself, Pete thought, Chinese.

"I'm from the earth and not superior to mortals," the pot Oh Ho continued, in a conversational way. "I'm not above identifying myself. Always beware of manifestations too lofty to identify themselves. You are Peter Sands; I am Oh Ho. What you saw, that figure holding that large ancient volume, that was an entity of the noosphere, from the Seas of Knowledge, who come down here all the way from Sumerian times. As Therapeutae they assisted the Greek healer Asclepiades; as spirits or plasmic lifeforms of wisdom they called themselves 'Thoth' to the Egyptians, and when they built— they are excellent artificers—they were 'Ptath' to the Egyptians and 'Hephaestus' to the Greeks. They actually have no names at all, being a composite mind. But I have a name, just as you have. Oh Ho. Can you remember that? It's a simple name."

"Sure," Pete said. "Oh Ho, a Chinese name."

The pot wavered; it was shimmering away. "Oh Ho," it repeated. "Ho Oh. Oh, Oh, Oh. Ho On. Think of Ho On, Peter Sands, someday when you are talking with Dr. Abernathy. The little clay pot which came from the earth and can, like you, be smashed to bits and return to the earth, which lives only as long as your kind does."

" 'Ho On,' " Pete echoed dutifully.

"That which is benign will identify itself by name," Ho On said, invisible now; it was only a voice, a thinking, mentational entity which had possessed Pete's mind. "That which won't is not. We are alike, you and I, equals in a certain real way, made from the same stuff. Peter Sands. I have told you who I am; *and from old, I knew you.*"

What a silly name, he thought: Ho On. A silly name for a transitory, breakable pot. Well, he liked it anyhow; it had, as it said, treated him as an equal. And somehow that seemed more important than any vast transcendent significance which the weighty foreign words in the huge book might contain. Words he could not fathom anyhow; they were beyond him. He, like the clay pot Ho On, was too limited. But that *was* Jesus Christ I saw, he realized. I know it was Him. It *looked* like Him.

"Anything else you wish to know before I leave?" Ho On's thoughts came to him, within his head.

Pete Sands said, "Tell me the most important thing that, under any circumstance, could be told. But that's true."

Ho On thought, "St. Sophia is going to be reborn. She wasn't acceptable before."

He blinked. Who was St. Sophia? It was like telling him that St. Vitus was going to dance again . . . it was a joke. Keen disappointment filled him. It had simply ended up with something silly, like its name. And now he felt it leave . . . on that meager, if meaningless, note.

And then the drugs wore off. And he now no longer saw or heard; again he surveyed his living room, his familiar microtapes and projector, his tape-spools, and littered plastic desk; he saw Lurine smoking her pipe, he smelled the cavendish tobacco . . . his head felt swollen and he got up unsteadily, knowing that only an instant in real time had passed, and for Lurine nothing had occurred. Nothing had changed. And she was right.

This was not an event; Christ had not manifested Himself. What had occurred was that which Pete Sands had hoped for: an augmentation of his own faculties of perception.

"Jesus," he said aloud.

"What's the matter?" Lurine asked.

"I saw Him," he informed her. "He exists. To save us. He's always there, always will be, has always been." He walked into the kitchen and poured himself a small quantity, perhaps two thirds of a shot, of bourbon from the precious prewar bottle.

When he returned to the living room Lurine was reading a badly printed magazine, a mimeographed newsletter circulated from town to town here in the Mountain States area.

"You merely sit," he said, incredulous.

"What am I supposed to do? Clap?"

"But it's important."

"You saw it; I didn't." She continued reading the newsletter; it came from Provo, Utah.

"But He's there for you, too," Pete said.

"Good." She nodded absently.

He seated himself, feeling weak and nauseated; side-effects from the pills. There was silence and then Lurine spoke again, still absently.

"The Sows are sending the inc, Tibor McMasters, on a Pilg. To find the God of Wrath and capture his essence for their murch."

"What in god's name is a 'murch'?" SOW jargon; he did not ever understand.

"Church mural." She glanced up. "They speculate he'll have to travel well over a thousand miles; it's Los Angeles, I believe."

"You think I care?" he said furiously.

"I think," she said, laying aside the newsletter, then, and frowning thoughtfully, "that you ought to go along on the Pilg and then about fifty miles from here cut a leg off that cow that pulls Tibor's cart. Or short out his metabattery." She sounded perfectly, composedly serious.

"Why?"

"So he can't bring back the essence. For the mural."

"It couldn't matter less to me if—"

He broke off. Because someone had come to the door of his meager abode; he heard footsteps, then his dog Tom Swift And His Electric Magic Carpet barking. The bell clingled. Rising, he strode to the door.

Dr. Abernathy, his superior, the priest of the Charlottesville Combined Christian Church, stood there in his black cassock. "Is this too late to call on you?" Dr. Abernathy said, his round, small, bunlike face gracious in its formal concern not to be a bother.

"Come in." Pete held the door wide. "You know Miss Rae, Doctor."

"The Lord be with you," Dr. Abernathy said to her, nodding.

Immediately, correctly, she answered, "And with thy spirit." She rose. "Good evening, Doctor."

"I heard," Dr. Abernathy said, "that you are considering entering our church, taking confirmation and then the greater sacraments."

"Well," Lurine said, "I was—you know. Dissatisfied. I mean, who wants to worship the former Chairman of the ERDA?"

Dr. Abernathy passed into the tiny kitchen, and put the tea kettle on, to boil water for coffee. "You would be welcome," he said to her.

"Thank you, Doctor," Lurine said.

"But to be confirmed you would need half a year of

intensive religious instruction. On many topics: the sacraments, the rituals, the basic tenets of the Church. What we believe and also why. I hold adult-instruction classes two afternoons a week." He added, with a trace of embarrassment, "I have at present one adult receiving instruction. You could catch up very quickly; you have a bright, fertile mind. Meanwhile, you could attend services . . . however, you could not come to the rail, could not take Holy Communion; you realize that."

"Yes." She nodded.

"Have you been baptized?"

"I—" She hesitated. "Frankly, I don't know."

"We would baptize you with the special service for those who may have been baptized before. With *water*. Anything else—such as rose petals, as they used to do it before the war in Los Angeles—that does not count. By the way—I hear that Tibor is about to set forth on a Pilg. It's no secret, of course; my hearing of it verifies that. The Eltern of the Servants of Wrath, the rumor-mill says, have provided him with maps and photos and data, so that he can find Lufteufel. All I hope is that his cow holds out." Returning to the living room, he said to Pete Sands, "How about a little poker? Three does not seem to me enough, but we can play for genuine old copper cents. And no crazy games such as spit-in-the-ocean and baseball, just seven-card stud and straight and draw."

"Okay," Pete said, nodding. "But let's allow one wild card, dealer's choice, since there're only three of us."

"Fine," Dr. Abernathy said, as Pete walked off to get the deck and the box of chips. He drew a comfortable chair up to the table for Lurine Rae and then one for himself and at last one for Pete.

"And no chattering during the game," Pete said to Lurine.

They were dealing a hand of five-card draw, jacks or

better to open, when the cow-drawn cart of Tibor McMasters, battery-lamp sweeping ahead of it, pulled up at the door and tinkled its hopeful bell.

Studying his hand, Dr. Abernathy said thoughtfully in a preoccupied and abstracted way, "Um, I—uh—fold. So I'll go." He rose, to go to the door: to answer the presence of the well-known inc SOW artist.

On his cart, Tibor McMasters surveyed the progress of the poker game, and the conversation had that unique equal quality: everyone said as much as everyone else, although each player had his idiosyncratic mumble; and none of it, Tibor realized, meant anything—it was merely a noise, a banter, as their collective attention kept fixed on the play itself.

So only later, when a pause came, could he talk with Dr. Abernathy.

"Doctor." His voice, in his ears, sounded squeaky.

"Yes?" Abernathy said, counting his blue chips.

"You heard about the Pilg I've got to go on."

"Yep."

Tibor said, aware and thinking out his words, knowing intensely the meaning of them, "Sir, if I became a convert to Christianity, I wouldn't have to go."

At once Dr. Abernathy glanced up and said, scrutinizing him, "Are you really that much afraid?" Everyone else, Peter Sands and the girl, Lurine Rae, also stared at Tibor; he felt their motionless gaze.

"Yes," Tibor said.

"Often," Dr. Abernathy said, and took a fresh deck and began to riffle and vigorously shuffle the cards, "fear or dread is based on a sense of guilt, not experienced directly."

Tibor said nothing. He waited with the intention of lasting it out, however unpleasant and protracted it

might be. Priests, after all, were generally odd, intense
people, especially the Christian ones.

"You do not," Dr. Abernathy stated, "in your Ser
vants of Wrath Church, have either public or privat
confession."

"No, Doctor. But—"

"I will not try to argue or compete," Dr. Abernathy
said in a harsh, absolutely firm tone. "You are employed by Father Handy and it is his business if he
wants to send you."

"And yours," Lurine added, "if you want to quit or
go. Why not just quit?"

"And go," Tibor said, "into a vacuum."

"Always," Dr. Abernathy continued, "the Christian
Church is ready to accept anyone. Regardless of their
spiritual condition; it asks nothing of them except their
willingness. I would, however, suspect that what I can
offer you—I acting as a mouthpiece of God, not as a
man—is the opportunity for you to shirk your spiritual
duty . . . or, put more precisely, the opportunity to
acknowledge to yourself and to confess to me your deep
desire to shirk your spiritual duty."

"To a false church?" Lurine Rae protested, her dark
red eyebrows raised in astonishment. To Tibor she said
"They have a club; they're all members. It's what'
called 'professional ethics.' " She laughed.

"Why not make an appointment with me?" Dr. Aber
nathy asked Tibor. "I can accept your confession with
out your joining the Christian Church; it is not tied in
as the ancients put it."

With utmost caution, his mind very, very rapid in it
work, Tibor answered, "I—can't think of anything t
confess."

"You will," Lurine assured him. "He'll assist you
Even further."

Neither Dr. Abernathy nor Pete Sands said anything

and yet they seemed in some mysterious sense, perhaps by their mere passivity, to acknowledge what the woman said to be true. The father confessor knew his trade; like a good lawyer or doctor of medicine, Tibor reflected, he could draw his client out. Lead him and inform him. Find what was deep inside, hidden—not *plant* anything, but rather harvest it.

"Let me think this over," Tibor said. He felt entirely hesitant now. His intentions, his decision to do this as a solution to his horror at the idea of the soon-coming Pilg, seemed swamped with the second guesses of severe and fundamental doubt. What had seemed a good idea had been, to his disbelief, returned as unacceptable by the man who stood to benefit most—at least most after Tibor McMasters, who stood at the head of the line . . . for obvious reasons: reasons palpable to everyone in the room.

Confession? He felt no burden of guilt, no sting of death; he felt instead perplexed and afraid; that was all. Admittedly, he feared to a morbid and obsessive degree the proposed—in fact ordered—Pilg. But why did guilt have to come into it? The Gothic convolutions of this, the older church . . . and yet he had to admit that it somehow seemed appropriate, this interpretation of Dr. Abernathy's. Perhaps merely the unexpectedness of it alone had overwhelmed him; possibly that accounted for it.

Since he had nothing to say, the girl friend of Pete Sands naturally spoke up. "Confession," Lurine said meditatively, "is strange. You in no way feel free in the sense that you can sin again with license. Actually, you feel—" She gestured, as if they all really understood her—which Tibor did not. However, he nodded solemnly, as if he did. And took the opportunity—were they not discussing giddy, interesting subjects such as sin?—to scrutinize for the millionth time her sharply amplified breasts; she wore a shrunk-by-many-washings white cotton shirt and no bra, and in the shaded light of the living room her nipples cast a far, huge shadow on the far wall, each one in the process becoming enlarged to the size of a flashlight battery.

"You feel," Pete Sands declared, "your evil thoughts and deeds *articulated*. They take form and assume shapes. And are less fearsome because they become— just words, suddenly. Just the Logos. And," he added, "the Logos is good." He smiled, then, at Tibor, and now all at once the powerful thrust of Christian meaning struck at Tibor's mind. He in return felt soothed; he felt the healing rather than the philosophical quality of the older church: its doctrines admittedly made no sense, but neither did very much else in the world. Especially since the war.

Once more the three persons at the table, like a mundane and bisexual trinity, resumed their game. The discussion on the vital topic which he had come here for— vital at least to him—had terminated.

But then Dr. Abernathy said abruptly, lifting his eyes from the hand he held, "I could all of a sudden have *three* adults in my religious-instruction class. You, Miss Rae here, and the rather odd fellow currently attending, whom I know you all have met at one time or another, Walter Blassingame. Practically a renaissance of the primordial faith." His expression and tone held no evidence of his feelings—perhaps as a direct result of the game spread across the surface of the table.

Aloud, Tibor said, *"Erbarme mich, mein Gott."* By speaking in German he spoke to himself; as far as he knew, anyhow. But, to his amazement, Dr. Abernathy nodded, obviously understanding.

"The language," Lurine Rae said acidly, "of Krupp *und* Sohnen. Of I. G. Farben and A. G. Chemie. Of the

Lufteufel family all the way back to Adam Lufteufel—
or, more accurately, *Cain* Lufteufel."

Dr. Abernathy said to her, *"Erbarme mich, mein
Gott* is not the language of the German military estab-
lishment nor the industrial cartels. It's the *Klagenges-
chrei* of the human being, the human cry for help." He
explained to her and Peter Sands, "It means 'God save
me.'"

"Or 'God have mercy on me,'" Tibor said.

"Erbarmen," Dr. Abernathy said, "means 'to have
mercy,' except in that one phrase; it is an idiom. The
suffering is not from God; therefore God is not asked to
be merciful; He is asked to rescue you." He all at once,
then, threw down his cards. "Tomorrow morning at ten,
in my office, Tibor. I'll see you privately, explain a little about the act of confession, and then we'll go into
the chapel where the Reserve Sacrament is; you will of
course be unable to genuflect, but He will not hold that
against you. A legless man cannot kneel."

"All right, Doctor," Tibor agreed. And felt better,
strangely, even at this point. As if something had been
lifted from the sagging grasp of his combined manual
extensors, a load which overstrained the metabattery
and made the ominous black smoke rise from the trans-
former, gear box, and bank of selenoids of his cart.

And up to now he had not even known of its existence.

"My three queens," Dr. Abernathy informed Pete
Sands, "beat your two pairs. Sorry." He collected the
meager pot; Tibor saw that the minister's little pile of
chips was growing: he had been steadily winning.

"Can I play?" Tibor inquired.

The players glanced at one another in a mild way, as
if barely conscious of his presence, let alone his request.

"Takes a dollar—in silver bits—to buy in," Pete

said. He tossed one chip to an empty spot on the table. "That represents the dollar you owe the banker. Have you a dollar? And I don't mean in scrip."

The priest said mildly, "Show Tibor how you back up your talk, Pete. Show him your arsenal."

"This is how people can tell I'm never bluffing," Pete said. He dug down deep into his pocket and brought out a roll of dimes, so marked.

"Wow," Tibor said.

"I've never lost at blackjack," Pete said. "I just double my bets." He undid one end of the roll of dimes to show Tibor that within the brown paper actual silver coins existed: genuine money, from the old, old days.

"You sure you want to play?" Lurine Rae said, raising her eyebrow and eyeing Tibor. "Knowing this?"

He had, in his pocket, the one-third initial advance from the SOWers for the proposed murch. He had not spent a bit of it—just in case at some dreadful future hour of reckoning it had to be returned. Now, however, he took out six silver quarters, displayed them in the grip of his right manual-extensor's claws. And so, as he rolled his cart closer to the table, Pete Sands counted out the red and blue chips which his dollar and a half bought. It had now become a four-person—and hence a better—game.

FOUR

Later that night, after pretty red-haired Lurine Rae and Tibor McMasters on his cow cart had respectively walked and rolled off, Pete Sands elected to discuss his vision with Dr. Abernathy.

Dr. Abernathy did not approve. "If you keep on having visions, I'm going to advise you that you be forbidden to approach the rail."

"You'd cut me off from the greatest of the sacraments?" Pete could not believe it. Surely the short, roosterlike, red-faced, round little old priest was merely in a temporary—and for him quite normal—dark mood.

"Well, if you're having visions, you don't need the intercession of the priest and the saving power of the sacraments."

Pete said, "You want to know what He—"

"His appearance," Dr. Abernathy said, "is not a topography which I care to discuss, as if you'd seen a rare butterfly."

Plunging in, Pete said, "Receive my confession, then. Now." He knelt, hands clasped together, waited.

"I'm not dressed properly."

"Balls."

Dr. Abernathy sighed, departed, and presently returned in the white robes necessary; pulling a chair into place, he seated himself with his back to Pete. Then, crossing himself, after praying inaudibly, he said, "May Thy ears receive the humble confession of this, Thy servant, who has erred and wishes to be received back into Thy bountiful grace."

"Here's how He looked," Pete began.

Interrupting, Dr. Abernathy, slightly more loudly, prayed, "Cause this, Thy servant, now puffed up with vainglory and imagining in his dustlike ignorance that he has direct access to Thy Holy Presence through what is a chemical and magical process devoid of sanctification—"

"He is always there," Pete said.

"In confession," Dr. Abernathy said, "do not recount the actions of others, even of Him."

Pete declared, "I most humbly confess that I deliberately ingested drugs of an intricate nature for the purpose of transcending ordinary reality for a glimpse of the absolute, and this was wrong. Further, I confess that in all honesty. I believed in and still do believe in the veracity of my vision, that I genuinely saw Him, and if I am mistaken, I beg Him to forgive me, but if it *was* Him, then He must have wished—"

"From dust thou art come," Dr. Abernathy interrupted. "Oh man, how small thou art. Lord God, open this idiotic fool's inner heart to the wisdom of Thee: which is that no man can see Thee and announce predicate adjectives as to Thy appearance and being."

"I confess further," Pete said, "that I did harbor and still harbor resentment at being told to desist from my personal search for God, and that I believe that one man working alone can still find Him. Without the mediation of the priest, the sacraments, and the church; this I confess most humbly to believe and although I know it is wrong I nonetheless still believe it."

They sat in silence for an interval and then Pete Sands said, "Funny you should say that 'dust to dust' thing. It reminds me of what Ho On said about being made from the clay of the ground."

Dr. Abernathy stared at him fixedly.

"What's the matter?" Pete said uneasily.

" 'Ho On'?"

"Yes. In my vision—the ceramic pot gave that as its name. Silly pot, silly name. Must have been a silly hallucinogenic; probably had some of those wartime disorientation chemicals in it that—"

Dr. Abernathy said, in a surprisingly grave voice, "That is Greek."

"Greek!"

"I'm not positive of precision, but it's a name God gave Himself in the Bible, in the Greek part. Yahweh, as a Hebrew verb, means something in the older part, when He talks to Moses . . . it's a form of the verb 'to be'; it describes His nature. 'I am He Who causes to be,' is what Yahweh literally means. So that Moses could report back to his people the nature—that is, the ontology—of his God. But Ho On . . ." The priest pondered. "The Essence of Essence. The Most Holy? The On High? The Ultimate Power?"

Laughing, Pete said, "This was a little clay pot. Anyhow, as you say, I was tripping out on drugs. At first it said, 'Oh Ho,' and then it went, 'Oh, oh, oh,' and finally 'Ho On.' "

"But that is Greek."

Pete asked, "Who was St. Sophia?"

"There never was any St. Sophia."

At that, Pete started laughing in the fashion of a man joyfully flashing back to what had been a good drug trip. "No St. Sophia? A pot that calls itself God, and a revelation about a non-existent saint—that was some mixture I took. Once in a lifetime. You're right; it is black mass. A saint is going to be reborn—"

"I'll look it up," Dr. Abernathy said. "But I'm sure

there was no such saint. . . ." He departed for a time, then, abruptly, returned carrying a large old book with him, a reference book. "St. Sophia," he declared loudly, "was a building."

"A *building!*"

"A very famous building, destroyed of course during the smash. The emperor Justinian had it personally constructed. The name for it, Haggia Sophia, is Greek. Also Greek, like Ho On. It means 'the Wisdom of God.' She—it—is going to be reborn?"

"That's what Ho On told me," Pete said.

Seating himself, Dr. Abernathy said carefully, "What else did this Ho On, this ceramic pot, say to you?"

"Nothing important. It complained a lot. Oh yes: it said that St. Sophia hadn't been acceptable before."

"And you derived nothing more?"

"Well, nothing that—"

" 'Haggia Sophia,' " the priest said, "can also refer to the Word of God, and hence by extension is a cypher for Christ. It is a cypher within a cypher: Haggia Sophia; St. Sophia; the Wisdom of God; the Logos; Christ; and therefore, according to our Trinitarian beliefs, God. Read, ahem . . . ah: Proverbs 8:22–31. Most fascinating."

"A saint that never even existed," Pete said. "The pot put me on. It was a gag. It was pulling my leg."

"Are you still sleeping with Lurine Rae?" The priest's voice had a sudden, hardly expected sharpness to it; he blinked.

"Um, yes," Pete muttered.

"So this is the road our converts travel to reach us."

Pete said, "When you're losing you're losing. I mean, you take them as they come."

"I order you," Dr. Abernathy said, "to stop sleeping with that girl, whom you are not married to."

"If I do that she won't join the Christian Church."

There was silence. Each man regarded the other, heavily breathing; faces flushed, the two of them glared disapproval and masculine authority, with overtones of some deeper, higher mandate, obscurely articulated but nonetheless there.

"And the visions," Dr. Abernathy said. "It is time you gave them up as well. You confessed the use of vision-inducing drugs. I am instructing you to turn all such drugs over to me."

"Wh-wh-wh*at?*"

The priest nodded. "Right now." He held out his hand.

"I never should have confessed." His voice trembled and he could not, for the life of him, keep it steady. "Listen," he said, "how about a deal? I'll stop sleeping with Lurine, but you let me keep—"

Dr. Abernathy stated, "I am more concerned with the drugs. There is a satanic element involved, a vitiated but still-real black mass."

"You're"—Pete gestured—"out of your mind!"

The hand remained. Waiting.

" 'Black mass.' " Disgusted, he said, "Some deal. I can't win; I either—" Too much, he thought gloomily. What a mistake it had been to slip over into the formal relationship with Abernathy; the priest had ceased to be a man, had assumed transcendent power. "Penance," he said aloud. "You've got me. Okay; I have to give up my whole goddamn supply of medication. What a victory for you, tonight. What a reason for joining the Christian Church; you have to give away everything you like, even the search for God! You sure don't want converts very bad—as a matter of fact, it strikes me as weird, the way you discouraged McMasters; my god, you as much as told him right flat to his face that he ought to go back to Handy and do his job and *not* be a convert. Is that what you want? For him to stay there with the

SOWers and go on his Pilg, which he's trying so darn
hard to get out of? What a way to run a church; no
wonder you're losing out, like I said."

Dr. Abernathy continued to extend his open hand,
waiting.

Just that one thing, Pete Sands reflected. Not picking
up when the inc asked to join us so as not to go on the
Pilg; why didn't you pick up on that? It wasn't that difficult a decision; normally, Dr. Abernathy would have
conscripted Tibor into the Christian Church instantly:
Pete Sands had witnessed such abrupt total conversions
many times.

"I'll tell you what," Pete said aloud. "I'll turn over
my supply of medication to you if you'll tell me why
you blocked McMasters when he tried to duck in here.
Okay? A deal?"

"He should have courage. He should stand up to the
duties imposed on him. Even by a false and profane
mimic-church."

"Aw, you must be kidding." It still rang wrong; in
fact even more so, now. Asked outright for his reason,
Dr. Abernathy revealed that he had no reason. Or
rather, Pete realized musingly, he isn't telling.

"The drugs," Dr. Abernathy said. "I told you why I
abstained from the temptation of enticing one of the finest murch painters in the Rocky Mountain area into the
Church of Christ; now give me——"

"Anything," Pete Sands said quietly.

"Pardon?" Blinking, Dr. Abernathy cupped his ear.
"Oh, I see. Anything else instead of the——medication."

"Lurine and anything else," Pete said in a voice that
almost refused to be heard; he was in fact unsure
whether the priest had caught all the words or only the
tone. But the tone by itself; that would convey everything. In all his life, even during the war, he had never
sounded quite like that. At least so he hoped.

"Hmm," Dr. Abernathy said. " 'Lurine and anything else.' Rather a grandiose offer. You must have become habituated to one or more of your drugs; correct?" He eyed Pete keenly.

"Not the drugs," Pete said, "but that which the drugs show me."

"Let me think." Dr. Abernathy pondered. "Well, nothing enters my mind tonight . . . possibly it would be worth shelving for now; I can perhaps stipulate some alternative tomorrow or the day after."

And not only this, Pete thought, but you also won all the silver I had on me when we began the game tonight. Jeez.

"By the way," Dr. Abernathy said. "How *is* Lurine in bed? Are her breasts, for example, as firm as they appear?"

"She's like the tides of the sea," Pete said gloomily. "Or the wind that sweeps across the plain. Her breasts are like mounds of chicken fat. Her loins—"

Grinning, Dr. Abernathy said, "In any case, it's been a pleasure for you to have known her. In the biblical sense."

"You really want to know how she is? Average. And after all, I've had plenty of women. Lots of them were better lays, and lots of them worse," Pete said. "That's all."

Dr. Abernathy continued to grin.

"What's funny?" Pete demanded.

"Perhaps it's the way hungry men speak of smorgasbords," Dr. Abernathy replied.

Pete reddened, knowing the flush would reach the crown of his head, all visible.

He shrugged and turned away. "What's it to you?"

"Curiosity," said Dr. Abernathy, scratching his chin and pulling his smile straight. "I'm a curious man, and even secondhand carnal knowledge *is* knowledge."

"And perhaps too many years in the confessional promote a certain voyeurism," Pete observed.

"If so, this in no way vitiates the sacrament," said Dr. Abernathy.

"I know about the Waldensians," said Pete. "What I said was—"

"—That I'm a peeping Tom." Dr. Abernathy sighed and rose, adjusting his cassock as he stood. "Okay, I'll be going now."

Pete accompanied him to the door, letting Tom Swift And His Electric Magic Carpet out at the same time, for his usual evening business.

The dust fought the dew and the former settled to the ground, save for that raised by the cow and kicked back into his face. Tibor turned his head to the side and regarded the colors of morning.

The colors . . . Christ! the colors! he thought. In the morning everything lives in a special way—the wet-green leaves and the oily grayblue of the jay's feathers—the brownwetblack of the road-apple—everything! Everything is special until about eleven o'clock. Then the color is still there, but a certain magic is gone out of the word, a wet magic. There was a faint haze in the western corner of the nine-thirty world. He thought of all the shadows in all the Rembrandt repros he had seen. So easy to fake, that man, he thought. They talk of the Rembrandt eyes. What ever do they see? Whatever they want. Because there is nothing there but shadows. He was not a morning painter, so he would be easy to fake. But all those wetmorning people, the impressionists—lumped together perhaps only because they sat in the same corner of the Café Gaibois—they would be harder to emulate. They saw something like this and drew perfect circles about it.

He watched the birds and digested their flight. It was

too good a morning. He etched it within his mind. He did it in watercolors. He did it in oils, the hard way, layer by painful layer.

To keep something else out, he did it.

What?

The cow made a soft, lowing noise and he murmured to her as softly.

God! how he hated to work by artificial light! It was sufficient for pieces, for corners and borders, for supporting material, but the final product—*das Dinge selber*—this must be a thing of *Morgen*.

And his mind came back, full circle, and the morning and the colors went away, for a time.

Dr. Abernathy's place was over the hill and around the corner, and then about a mile. By ten o'clock, at this pace, he would be at the front door. What then? He tried to block the thought by sketching a tree, in his mind. But autumn came down upon it, the leaves withered and fell, were swept away. What then?

It was a thing that had taken him suddenly, the notion of a God of mercy and love. Only a few days ago, as a matter of fact. If they'd take him in and baptize him, he would not even have to be shrived, as he understood it. Not to be confused with the heretical notions of the Anabaptists, he realized with a certain pleasure that this would relieve him of the necessity of confessing to the thoughts he had held, of Helen, with the breasts like clouds, Lurine, with the skin like milk, Fay, with the mouth like honey, of the paint he had diverted to his own use, of the blocks of stone he had stolen to sculpt.

What would Dr. Abernathy say? Oh, hell! He would counsel him, give him a catechism to study, test him later, baptize him, admit him as a communicant.

What was it then that broke the morning?

The night before, he had dreamed of his mural. Carl Lufteufel was a vacuum in the middle, crying out to be filled. The face in the repro which Dominus McComas had shown him always looked slightly past him. Not really at him. Not yet. Once he saw the man and captured the eyes—not hidden like those of a Rembrandt, no!—but the eyes of the God of Wrath, actually focused upon him, and all the slack/tightened/flaccid muscles of That Face, the bags or black smudges under the eyes, the parallelograms of the brow—all these things—once they were turned upon him, if only for a morning's instant, then that vacuum would be filled. Once he saw it, all the world would see it—by his seeing and the six fingers of his steel hand.

He spat, licked his lips, and coughed. The morning was too much with him.

The Holstein—Darlin' Corey—turned the corner, and then about a mile remained.

He moved slowly into the study and regarded the priest.

"Thank you," Tibor said, accepting a cup of coffee and manipulating it slowly into a position allowing two quick, scalding sips.

Dr. Abernathy added cream and sugar to his own and stirred noisily.

They sat awhile in silence, then Dr. Abernathy said, "You want to become a Christian." Whatever question mark may have followed the sentence was a thing implied only, by a slight raising of the eyebrows.

"I am—interested. Yes. As I said last night—"

"Yes, yes, I know," said Dr. Abernathy. "Needless to say, I am pleased that our example has impressed you in this fashion." He turned away then and stared out his window and said, "Can you believe in God the Father Almighty, Creator of Heaven and Earth, and in his only begotten son Jesus Christ our Lord, born of the virgin Mary, who suffered under Pontius Pilate, was crucified, died, and was buried, and on the third day rose again?"

"I think so," said Tibor. "Yes, I think so."

"Do you believe He will come to judge the living and the dead?"

"I can, if I try," Tibor said.

"You're an honest man, anyhow," Dr. Abernathy said. "Now, despite the rumor that we're looking for business, we're not. I'd love to welcome you to the fold, but only if you're sure that you know what you're doing. For one thing, we're poorer than the Servants of Wrath. So, if you're looking for business here, forget it. We can't afford murals or even illuminated manuscripts."

"That was the farthest thing from my mind, Father," said Tibor.

"All right," said Dr. Abernathy. "I just wanted to be sure that we were meeting on the same ground."

"I'm certain that we are," said Tibor.

"You're in the employ of the SOWs," said Dr. Abernathy, pronouncing each letter.

"I've taken their money," said Tibor. "I've a job to do for them."

"What do you think of Lufteufel, really?" asked Dr. Abernathy.

"A difficult subject," said Tibor, "since I've never seen him. I have a need to paint from experience. A photograph—such as the one they furnished me—it would do only if I could lay eyes on the man himself, if but for an instant."

"What do you think of him as God?" asked Dr. Abernathy.

"I don't know," said Tibor.

". . . As man?" asked Dr. Abernathy.

"I don't know."

"If you have doubts, then why do you wish to switch at this point in the game?" Dr. Abernathy asked. "Perhaps it would be better to resolve them within the context where they arose."

"Your religion has something more to offer," said Tibor.

"Like what?" asked Dr. Abernathy.

"Love, faith, hope," said Tibor.

"Yet you're taking their money," Dr. Abernathy said.

"Yes," said Tibor. "I've already made an agreement with them."

"One which requires a Pilg?" Dr. Abernathy asked.

"Yes," said Tibor.

"If you convert today, what will you do about this commission?" asked Dr. Abernathy.

"Give it up," said Tibor.

"Why?" Dr. Abernathy inquired.

"Because I don't want to make the Pilg," said Tibor.

They both sipped their coffee.

Finally, "You think you're being an honest man," said Dr. Abernathy. "One who meets all his commitments. Yet you want to come over to us in order to break faith with them."

Tibor looked away. "I could give them back the money," he said.

"True," said Dr. Abernathy, "as it is commanded, 'Thou shalt not steal.' This applies to the SOWs, as well as anyone else—so it is only just that either you give it back or keep your promise and paint the mural. On the other hand, what is it they have really asked you to do?"

"A mural involving the God of Wrath," said Tibor.

"Just so," said Dr. Abernathy. "And where does God live?"

"I do not understand," said Tibor, sipping his coffee.

"Is it not true that He dwells in all places and all times, as eternity is His home?" asked Dr. Abernathy.

"I think the SOWs and the Christians both agree on this point."

"I believe so," said Tibor. "Only, as God of This World—"

"Well, He might be found anywhere," said Dr. Abernathy.

"Father, I fail to follow you," said Tibor.

"What if you do not succeed in locating Him?" asked Dr. Abernathy.

"Then I should be unable to complete the mural," said Tibor.

"And what would you do then?" asked Dr. Abernathy.

"Continue with what I've been doing," said Tibor, "painting signs, painting houses. I'd give back the money, of course—"

"Why need you resort to this extreme? Since God—if *he* be God—may be found anywhere, this being his world, it would seem you might properly seek him there," said Dr. Abernathy.

With a certain uneasiness, and yet a glimmer of fascination, Tibor said, "I'm afraid I still don't see what you mean, sir."

"What if you saw his face in a cloud?" said Dr. Abernathy. "Or in the shiftings of the Great Salt Lake, at night, under the stars? Or in a fine mist descending just as the heat of day departed?"

"Then it would only be a guess," said Tibor, "a—a fake."

"Why?" asked Dr. Abernathy.

"Because I'm only mortal," said Tibor, "and therefore liable to error. If I were to guess, I might guess wrong."

"Yet if it be his will that this thing be done, would he allow this error?" asked Dr. Abernathy in a strong, measured voice. "Would he allow you to paint the wrong face?"

"I don't know," said Tibor. "I don't think so. But—"

"Then why don't you save yourself much time, effort, and grief," said Dr. Abernathy, "and proceed in this manner?"

After a pause, Tibor murmured, "I don't feel it would be right."

"Why not?" said Dr. Abernathy. "He could really be anyone, you know. Chances are, you'll never find the real Carl Lufteufel."

"Why not?" said Tibor. "Because it wouldn't be right, that's why. I've been commissioned to paint the God of Wrath in the center of the mural—in appropriate lifelike authentic colors—so it is therefore important to know him as he really is."

"*Is* it all that important?" said Dr. Abernathy. "How many people knew his appearance in the old days? And if they are living, how many of them would recognize him today—*if* he be still living, that is?"

"It's not that," said Tibor. "I know I could fake it, that I could manufacture a face—just from the repro I've seen. The thing of it is, though, it wouldn't be true."

"True?" said Dr. Abernathy. "True? What's truth? Would it detract from a single SOW's devotion were he to look upon the *wrong* face, so long as his feeling were proper in terms of his faith? Of course not. I'm not trying to denigrate those you may consider my competitors. Far from it. It is you that I value. A Pilg is a risky thing at best. What would be gained by losing you? Nothing. What would be lost by losing you? A soul and a good painter, perhaps. I should hate to lose you on a matter of such small consequence."

"It is *not* a matter of small consequence, Father," said Tibor. "It is a matter of honesty. I have been paid to do a thing, and by God!—yours or theirs—I must do it properly. This is the way that I work."

"Peace," said Dr. Abernathy, raising his hand. He took another sip of coffee, then said, "Pride, too, is a sin. For by this, Lucifer fell from heaven. Of all the Deadly Seven, Pride is the worst. Anger, Avarice, Envy, Lust, Sloth, Gluttony—these represent man's relationships to others and the world. Pride, however, is absolute. It represents the subjective relationship of a person to himself. Therefore, it is the most mortal of them all. Pride requires nothing of which to be proud. It is the ultimate in narcissism. I feel, perhaps, that you are a victim of such sentiments."

Tibor laughed. Then he gulped coffee.

"I fear you have the wrong man," he said. "I've precious little of which to be proud." He placed the coffee cup before him and raised his metal hand. "You would call *me* proud—of anything? Hell! I'm half machine, sir! Of all the sins you've named, it's probably the one with least application."

"I wouldn't bet money on it," said Dr. Abernathy.

"I came to discuss religion with you," said Tibor.

"That's true," said Dr. Abernathy, "that's true. I think that that is what we are discussing. I am trying to place your task in proper perspective before you. More coffee?"

"Yes, please," said Tibor.

Dr. Abernathy poured and Tibor looked out the window. Eleven o'clock, that moment of truth, was passing over the world, he knew. For something had just gone out of it. What it was, he would never know.

He sipped and thought back upon the previous evening.

"Father," he said, finally, "I don't know who's right or wrong—you or them—and maybe I'll never know. But I can't cheat somebody when I tell them I'm going to do a thing. If it had been the other way around, I'd give you the same consideration."

Dr. Abernathy stirred and sipped. "And maybe we wouldn't really have cared if you could not have found us the Christ for our *Last Supper*," he said, "so long as you did a good job. I am not trying to dissuade you from doing what you think is right. It is just that I think that you are wrong, and you could make things a lot easier on yourself."

"I'm not asking for easy things, Father."

"You are making me sound like something I am not trying to be," said Dr. Abernathy. "It is only, I repeat, that I think there is a way in which you could make things easier on yourself."

"In other words, you want me to go away for a time, pretend to have seen the face I should see, paint it, and be done with it," said Tibor.

"To be quite frank about it," said Dr. Abernathy, "yes. You would be cheating no one—"

"Not even myself?" asked Tibor.

"Pride," said Dr. Abernathy, "pride."

"I'm sorry, sir," said Tibor, lowering his coffee cup. "I'm sorry, but I can't do it."

"Why not?" asked Dr. Abernathy.

"Because it wouldn't be right," said Tibor. "I'm not that sort of man. As a matter of fact, your suggestions have given me second thoughts about your religion. I believe I'd like to postpone my decision with respect to converting."

"As you would," said Dr. Abernathy. "Of course, by our teachings, your immortal soul will be in constant jeopardy."

"Yet," said Tibor, "you may consider no man damned, isn't that right?"

"That is true," said Dr. Abernathy. "Who gave you that Jesuitical bit of knowledge?"

"Fay Blaine," said Tibor.

"Oh," Dr. Abernathy said.

"Thank you for your coffee, sir," said Tibor. "I believe I'd better be going. . . ."

"May I give you a catechism?—something to read along the way?"

"Yes, thank you."

"You don't like me or respect me, do you, Tibor?"

"Let me reserve my opinion, Father."

"Reserve it, then, but take this," said Dr. Abernathy.

"Thank you," said Tibor, accepting the pamphlet.

Dr. Abernathy said, "I will disclose something more to you which you should know. I came across it in a textbook about the religions of the ancient Greeks. Their god Apollo was a god of constancy, and when tested he always was found to be the same. This was a major quality in him; he was what he was . . . always. In fact, one could define Apollo by this, and the Apollonian personality in humans." He coughed and went on rapidly, "But Dionysus, the god of unreason, was the god of metamorphosis."

"What is 'metamorphosis'?" Tibor asked.

"Change. From one form to another. Thus you see, the God of Wrath, also being a god of unreason, like Dionysus, can be expected to hide, to camouflage himself, to conceal, *to be what he is not;* can you imagine worshiping a god who, rather than is, is what he is not?"

Tibor gazed at him in perplexity. Perplexity, the efforts of two ordinary men, filled the room: perplexity, not understanding.

"These sayings are hard," Dr. Abernathy said, at last. He rose to his feet. "I'll see you again on your return?"

"Perhaps," said Tibor, activating his cart.

"The Christian God—" Dr. Abernathy hesitated, seeing how worn Tibor looked, worn by perplexity. "He is the God of unchange. 'I am what I am,' as God puts it to Moses, in the Bible. That is our God."

Outside, all magic had fled from the noonday world, the sun had hidden its face behind a brief cloud, and Darlin' Corey had eaten a bumblebee and was ill.

FIVE

He returned to the digs the following afternoon. The door grumbled when he inserted his finger, but it recognized the loops and whorls and slid halfway to the right. He sidled through and kicked it, and it closed behind him.

Adjusting his side-pack, which contained a new supply of herbicides, he paused for a moment to touch the lump which had grown between his left temple and forehead. It throbbed, it drove a shaft of pain through his head, as he knew it would. But he could not keep his hands away from it. The sore-tooth reaction, he decided.

He gulped another tablet from his new supply, knowing that it would have less than the desired effect.

Turning, then, he moved down the perpetually lit, perpetually poorly lit tunnel that led to the bunkers. Before he reached the one in which he was currently sleeping, his foot came down atop a small red truck and he was pitched forward to land upon his shoulder. As he fell, he shielded his aching head with an upflung arm. Activated by the push of his foot, the truck blew its horn and raced back up the tunnel.

After a moment, a short, heavyset figure raced past him, making sobbing noises.

"Tuck! Tuck!" it cried, pursuing the sound of the horn.

He raised himself to his knees, then to his feet. Staggering through the doorway, he noted that, as he had suspected, the room was now a shambles. Tomorrow I'll move into the next one, he decided. It's easier than cleaning the damned things out.

He dropped his pack upon the nearest table and collapsed onto the bed, pressing the back of his right wrist to his forehead.

A shadow across his eyelids told him that he was no longer alone. Without opening his eyes or changing his position, he snarled, "Alice, I told you to keep your toys out of the hall! I gave you a nice box for them! If you don't start keeping them there, I'm going to take them all away from you."

"No!" said the high-pitched voice. "Tuck . . ."

Then he heard the slap of her bare feet upon the floor, and the lid of the toy box creaked. It was too late to cry out, and knowing what was coming next, he gritted his teeth as she let it fall shut with a crash that bounced from all the walls of his sparse cell and converged upon his head.

The fact that she doesn't know any better doesn't alter the difficulty, he decided. Three weeks before, he had brought Alice home to the digs—an idiot girl whom the inhabitants of Stuttgart had expelled from their midst. Whether out of sympathy for her condition or the desire for companionship, he could not say. Probably something of both had entered into his choice. He could see now why they had done what they had done. She was impossible—maddening—to live with. As soon as he felt better, he would return her to the place where he had found her, crying beside the river with her dress caught in a thorn bush.

"Sorry," he heard her say. "Sorry, Daddy."

"I'm not your daddy," he said. "Eat some chocolate and go to sleep—please. . . ."

He felt like a glass of ice water. Crazy thought! The perspiration appeared like condensation now, while inside he was cold, cold, cold! He crossed his arms and began shaking. Finally, his fingers picked at the blanket, caught it, drew it over him.

He heard Alice singing to herself across the room, and for some reason this soothed him slightly.

Then, and the horrible part was that he knew he was not yet fully delirious, he was back in his office and his secretary had just rushed in with a sheaf of papers like a flower in her pink-nailed hand and she was talking and talking and talking, excitedly, and he was answering and nodding, shaking his head and gesturing, pushing Hold buttons on his telephones, stroking his nose, tugging his earlobe, and talking and not hearing or understanding a word that either of them was saying, not even hearing the ringing of the telephones, under whose buttons the little lights kept winking on and off, and there was a sense of urgency and a strange feeling of separation, removal, futility, while Dolly Reiber—that was her name—talked until suddenly he noted, quite academically, that she had the head of a dog and was beginning to howl (this he was able to hear, though faintly), and he smiled and reached out to stroke her muzzle and she became Alice-at-his-bedside.

"I told you to go to sleep!" he said.

"Sorry, Daddy," she told him.

"It's all right! Go to sleep, like I told you."

The figure withdrew, and he found the strength to unsnap his ammo belts and tear off his clothing, for he no longer felt like a glass of ice water, and he pushed these items over the edge of the bed.

He lay there panting, and his head throbbed with each beat of his heart.

The rats! The rats . . . They were all around him, moving closer. . . . He reached for the napalm. But,

Deliver us, deliver us from Your Wrath, said the rats, and he chuckled and ate their offerings. "For a time," he told them, and then the sky burst and there were slow-swimming, shapeless forms all about him, mainly red, though some were colorless, and he existed indifferently as they flowed by him, and then—or before or after, he could not be certain, and he knew that it did not matter—he heard and felt, rather than saw, a light within his head, pulsing, and it was a pleasant thing and he let it soak deep into him for a time, for a time that could have been hours or seconds (it did not matter), and while he felt, suddenly, that his lips had been moving, he had heard no words, there where he was, until a voice said, "What's a D-III, Daddy?"

"Sleep, damn you! Sleep!" his mouth finally communicated to his ear, and there came the sound of fleeing footsteps. Rats . . . Deliver us . . . D-III . . . Light . . . Light. Light!

He was glowing like a neon tube, pulsing like one, too. Brighter and brighter. Red, orange, yellow. White! White and blinding! He reeled in the pure white light. Reveled in it for a moment. A moment only.

It descended slowly, and he saw it coming. He saw it hovering. He cowered, cringed, abased himself before it, but it began its eternally slow descent nevertheless. "God!" came the strangled cry from his entire being, but it drew nearer, nearer, was upon him.

A crown of iron came down, settled upon his brow, drew tighter, fit him. It tightened and felt like a circlet of dry ice about his head. Arms? Did he have arms? If so, he used them to try to drag it away, but to no avail. It clung there and throbbed, and he was back in his bunker in the digs, feeling it.

"Alice!" he cried out. "Alice! Please . . . !"

"What, Daddy? What?" as she came to him again.

"A mirror! I need a mirror! Get the little one on top of the john and bring it to me! Hurry!"

"Mirror?"

"Looking-glass! Spiegel! Reflector! The thing you see yourself in!"

"Okay." And she ran off.

"And a knife! I'll need a knife, I think!" he called out, not knowing whether he had been heard.

After an aching time, she returned. "I have the mirror," she said.

He snatched it from her and held it up. He turned his head and looked into it with his left eye.

It was there. A black line had appeared in the center of the lump.

"Listen, Alice," he said, and stopped then to draw a deep breath. "Listen . . . In the kitchen . . . You know the drawer where we keep the knives and forks and spoons?"

"I think . . . Maybe . . ."

"Go get it. Pull the whole drawer out—very carefully. Don't drop it. Then bring the whole thing here to me. Okay?"

"Kitten. Things drawer. Kitten. Things drawer. Things drawer . . ."

"Yes. Hurry, but be careful not to drop it."

She ran off, and a moment later he heard the crash and the rattling. Then he heard her whimpers.

He threw his feet over the edge of the bed and collapsed upon the floor. Slowly, he began to crawl.

He reached the kitchen and left moist handprints upon the tile. Alice cowered in the corner, repeating, "Don't hit, Daddy. Sorry, Daddy. Don't hit, Daddy . . ."

"It's all right," he said. "You can have another piece of chocolate." And he picked up two sharp knives of different sizes, turned, and began the long crawl back.

Ten minutes perhaps, and his hands were steady

enough to raise the mirror in the left and the small knife in the right. He bit his lip. The first cut will have to be a quick one, he decided, and he positioned the knife beneath the black line.

He slashed and screamed, almost simultaneously.

She ran to his side, sobbing, but he was sobbing too, and unable to answer.

"Daddy! Daddy! Daddy!" she cried.

"Give me my shirt!" he cried.

She pulled it from the pile of his clothing and dropped it on him.

He touched it gingerly to his brow, wiped the tears from his eyes on its sleeve. He bit his lip again, and from the wet trickle realized that it, too, needed wiping. Then, "Listen, Alice," he said. "You've been a good girl, and I'm not mad at you."

"Not mad?" she asked.

"Not mad," he said. "You've been good. Very good. But you've got to go away tonight and sleep in another room. This is because I'm going to be hurting and making noises, and there is going to be lots of blood—and I don't want you to see all this, and I don't think you'd like it either."

"Not mad?"

"No. But please go to the old room. Just for tonight."

"I don't like it there."

"Just for tonight."

"Okay, Daddy," she said. "Kiss me?"

"Sure."

And she leaned forward, and he managed to turn his head so that she did not hurt him. Then she withdrew, without—thank god!—undue noise.

She was, he estimated, around twenty-four years old, and, despite her wide shoulders and her fat-girded waist, was possessed of a face not unlike one of Rubens's cherubs.

After she had gone, he rested awhile, then raised the mirror once again. The blood was still coming, so he blotted it—several times—as he studied the wound. Good! he decided. The first cut had gone deep. Now, if he'd the guts . . .

He took up the knife and positioned it above the black line. Something inside him—down at that animal level where most fears are born—cried out, but he managed to ignore it for the single instant necessary to make the second cut.

Then both mirror and knife fell upon the bed and he grasped the shirt to his face. He blacked out then. No lights. No crown. Nothing.

How long it took him to come around, he did not know. But he pulled the shirt from his face, winced, licked his lips.

Finally, he raised the mirror and regarded himself.

Yes, he had succeeded in parenthesizing the thing. The first step had been completed. Now he would have to do some digging.

And he did. Each time the blade struck against the protruding piece of metal, his head felt like the inside of a cathedral bell, and it was minutes before he could proceed again. He kept mopping the blood and tears and sweat from his face.

Then it was there.

He had finally exposed a sufficient edge so that his fingernails might gain purchase. Biting his tongue now, as he had bitten his lower lip clean through, he took hold very gently, tightened his grip carefully, and pulled with all his strength.

When he awakened and was able to raise the mirror once again, it stood out a quarter of an inch from his head.

He moistened the shirt with his saliva in order to clean his face.

Again, the slow approach and the spasmodic tug. Again, the blackness.

After the fifth time, he lay there with a two-inch thorn of metal fallen from his right hand upon the bed, and his face was a sweating, bleeding, crying mask with a hole in the left side of it, and he slept a sleep without dreams—in fact, beneath that ruddy surface there seemed a certain layer of peace, though it could have been a trick of the lights through the mess.

She tiptoed in with the exaggerated care of a child, and raised both hands to her mouth and bit the knuckles because she knew that she was not supposed to bother him and she felt that if she cried she would.

But, it was like Halloween—like a mask, that he was wearing. She saw the shirt fallen to the floor. He was so wet . . .

"Daddy . . ." she whispered, and laid it across his face, pressing lightly, lightly, with fingertips like spiders' legs, until it absorbed all, all, all of that which covered him like mud or swarming insects.

Later, she pulled it away, because she had been cut, many times, and she knew that such things dry and stick and hurt to pull away.

He looked cleaner then, though still somewhat altered, and she clutched it to her and took it back with her, back to the old room, because it was his, because he had given her toys and chocolate and because she wanted something of his which he would not want anymore—not when it was that dirty.

Later, much later, when she looked at it, fully unrolled, spread out upon her bed, she was delighted to see that it bore a perfect likeness of his face, traced in the juices of his own body, lying there flat, dark now, conforming in every detail to his countenance. . . .

Save for the eyes—which, strangely, seemed horizontal—just slots—as though they viewed straight across the surface of the world, as if the world were flat and his gaze traveled on without end, forever.

She did not like the way it showed his eyes, so she folded it up and took it back and hid it away at the bottom of her toy box, forgetting it forever after.

This time, for some reason, she remembered not to drop the lid, but closed it carefully.

SIX

Here! The scrabbling man on hands and knees in the drainage ditch. Dark eyes seeking an opening. An X of canvas belts upon his back. Above him the lightnings, upon him the rain. And about the next bending of his way, he watches/they watch/it watches, for he/they/it —it—knows that he is coming with a pain in his head. And it glances into the place where the storm meets the earth and the mud is born, wipes splashes from its coat, sniffs the air, sees the man's head and shoulders pass the turning point, withdraws.

The man finds the opened sewer and crawls within.

After twenty feet he flicked on his hand torch and shone it upon the ceiling. He stood then on the walkway beside the slop and leaned his back against the wall. Mopping his brow on his khaki sleeve, he shook droplets from his hair and dried his hands on his trousers.

For a moment, he grimaced. Then, dipping into a shoulder-pack, he withdrew a tube of tablets, gulped one. The thunders echoed about him in that place and he cursed, clutching his temples. But it came again and again, and he fell to his knees, sobbing.

The level of the slop in the center ditch began to rise. Observing it in the light of his torch, he rose to his feet and staggered further inward until he came to something resembling a platform. The smell of refuse was more powerful here, but there was space to sit down with his back to the wall, so he did. He switched off the torch.

After a time, the pill began to take effect and he sighed.

See how feeble it is that has come among me.

He unsnapped his holster and thumbed down the safety catch on his revolver.

It has heard me and knows fear.

Then, between the rumbles of thunder there was only silence. He sat there for perhaps an hour, then drifted into a light sleep.

That which awakened him might have been sound. If so, it had been too soft to have registered consciously.

It is awake. How is it that it can hear me? Tell me. How is it that it can hear me?

"I can hear you," he said, "and I'm armed," his mind automatically falling to the weapon at his side and his finger finding its trigger.

(*Image of a pistol and feeling of derision as eight men fall before it clicks upon an empty chamber.*)

With his left hand he turned on the torch once more. As he swept it about, several opallike sparkles occurred in a corner.

Food! he thought. I'll need something before I make it back to the bunker! They'll do.

You will not eat me.

"Who are you?" he asked.

You think of me as rats. You think of a thing known as The Air Force Survival Handbook, *where it explains that if you cut off one of my heads—which is where the poison is—you must then slit open the ventral side and continue the cuts to extend the length of each leg. Subsequent to this, the skin can be peeled off, the belly*

*opened and emptied, the backbone split and both halves
roasted on sharpened sticks over a small fire.*

"That is essentially correct," he said, then. "You say
that you are 'rats'? I do not understand. The plural—
that's what I don't understand."

I am all of us.

He continued to stare at the eyes located about
twenty-five feet from him.

*I know now how you hear me. There is pain, pain in
you. This, somehow, lets you hear.*

"There are pieces of metal in my head," he said,
"from when my office exploded. I do not understand
this thing either, but I can see how it may be involved."

*Yes. In fact, I see that one of the pieces nearer the
surface will soon work its way free. Then you must
break your skin with your claws and withdraw it.*

"I don't have claws—oh, my fingernails. Then that
must be what's causing these headaches. Another piece
is moving around. Fortunately, I can use my knife. That
time I had to claw one out was pretty bad."

What is a knife?

(Steel, sharp, gleaming, with a handle.)

Where does one get a knife?

"One has one, finds one, buys one, steals one, or
makes one."

*I do not have one, but I have found yours. I do not
know how to buy or steal or make one. So I will take
yours.*

And more opallike sparkles occurred, and more, and
more, and slowly they drifted forward, and he knew
that his gun was worthless.

There came a terrible pain within his head and white
flashes destroying his seeing. When it cleared, there were
thousands of rats all about him and he moved without
thinking.

He pulled the bulb from his ammo belt, withdrew the pin, and hurled the bulb into their midst.

For three pulsebeats nothing happened, except that they continued their advance.

Then there came a blinding solar-corona blaze, which did not diminish but persisted for many minutes. White phosphorus. He followed it with napalm. He chuckled as they burned and screamed and clawed at one another. At least, something within him was chuckling, some part of him. The rats fell back and there came another pain within his head. There was an especially violent throbbing in the vicinity of his left temple.

Do not do that again, please. I did not realize You to be such a thing as You are.

"I damned well *will* do it, if you try what you tried again."

I will not. I will bring forth of rats for You to eat. Of the young, fat ones. Only deliver us from Your wrath.

"Very well."

How many of rats do You desire?

"Six should do it."

They will be of the very best and plumpest.

They were brought before him, and he beheaded them, cleaned them, and roasted them over the sterno stove he carried in his pack.

Would You care for more of rats? I can give You all that You desire.

"No, I need no more," he said.

Are You certain? Perhaps six more?

"These have been sufficient, for now," he said.

You will remain until the storm stops?

"Yes," he said.

Then You will go away?

"Yes," he said.

Come back to me one day, please. I will always have

more rats for You to eat. I wish to have You come back.

. . . And deliver us from Your wrath, oh thing You name in Your pain as Carl Lufteufel.

"Perhaps," he said, smiling.

SEVEN

Aboard his cart, Tibor McMasters rode in style, with a flourish; pulled by the faithful cow, the cart rattled and bounced on, and miles of weedy pasture passed by, flat country with stalks rising, both tough and dry: this had become arid land, not fit for crops any longer. As he rolled forward, Tibor exulted; he had finally begun his Pilg and it would be a success; he knew it would.

He did not especially fear cutpurses and highwaymen, partly because no one bothered with the highways . . . he could rationalize this fear away, telling himself that since no traffic passed this way, how could there be highwaymen?

"O friends!" he declared aloud, translating into English the opening words of Schiller's *An die Freunde*. "Not these tones! On the contrary, let us sing of—" He paused, having forgotten the rest. God damn it, he said fiercely to himself, baffled by the tricks of his own mind.

The sun blazed down, hot as minnows skimming in the metallic surf, the tidal rise and fall of reality. He coughed, spat, and continued on.

Over everything, the sensual proximity of decay. Even the wild weeds possessed it, this abandonment. No one cared; no one did anything. *O Freunde*, he thought. *Nicht diese Töne. Sondern . . .*

What if there were highwaymen invisible now, due to

mutation? No; impossible. He clung to that. Noted, preserved, and maintained that. He did not have to fear men: only the wilderness threatened him. In particular he feared the real possibility of a rupture in the road. A few wide ruts and—his cart would not travel on. He could well die amid boulders. Not the best death, he reflected. And yet, not one of the worst.

The broken limbs of trees blocked the road ahead. He slowed down, squinted in the patterned sunlight, trying to make out what it was.

Trees, he decided. Felled at the start of the war. No one has removed them.

In his cart he coasted up to the first tree. A trail of rough pebbles and dirt led off to one side, skirting the fallen trees; the trail, on the far side, led back to the road. If he had been on foot, or riding a bicycle . . . but instead he rested on a large cart, much too cumbersome to navigate the trail.

"God damn it," he said.

He stopped his cart, listened to the dull whistle of wind sighing through the broken trees. No human voices. Somewhere far off, something barked, perhaps a dog, or if not that, then a large bird. Squawk, squawk, the sounds came. He spat over the side of his cart and once more surveyed the trail.

Maybe I can make it, he said to himself.

But suppose his cart got stuck?

Gripping the tiller of the cart, he jogged forward, and rumbled off the weed-cracked road and onto the dirt trail. His wheels spun anxiously, a high-pitched whirring sound, and clouds of brown dust whistled up in a dry geyser into the sky.

The cart had become stuck.

He did not get very far, he realized. But, all at once, he felt savage, almost nauseated, fear. A sour taste rose up within him, and his chest and arms burned red with humiliation. Stuck so soon: it humiliated him. Suppose someone saw him, here, caught in the dirt by the side of the collapsing road? They would jeer, he thought. At me. And go on. But—more likely they would assist me, he thought. I mean, it would be unreasonable to jeer. After all, have I become cynical about mankind? They'd help, of course. And yet his ears still burned with shame. To distract himself from his plight he got out a much-creased, oil-soaked Richfield map, and consulted it with an idea that he might find something of use.

He located himself on the map. Hardly a drop in the bucket, he discovered. I've only gone say thirty or thirty-five miles.

And yet this constituted a different world from the one he knew at Charlottesville. Another world only thirty miles away . . . perhaps one of a thousand dissimilar universes wheeling through sidereal time and space. Here and there on the map: names that once meant something. Now it had become a lunar map, with craters: vast potholes scooped out of the earth, down to bedrock. Almost below the soil level, where basalt flourished.

He flicked his whip at the cow, threw the mode-selector into reverse, and, gritting his teeth, rocked back and forth between forward one and reverse; the cart seethed as if on a wilderness of open sea.

The smell of burning oil, the clouds of dust raised . . . that was all. He groaned, and let up on the throttle. And here am I going to die, a part of his brain declared, and, instantly, he jeered—jeered at himself and his broken plight. He did not need anyone else; he could heap ridicule on himself single-handedly.

He clicked on his emergency bullhorn. Powered by the huge wet-cell battery of the cart, the bullhorn wheezed: his breath augmented. And now his voice.

"Now h-h-hear this!" he declared, and, from all around him, his voice amplified. "I am Tibor McMasters, on an official Pilg for the Servants of Wrath, Incorporated. I'm stuck. Could you give me a hand?" He shut off the bullhorn, listened. Only the lisping of the wind in the tall weeds to his right. And, everywhere, the flat orange luminosity of the sun.

A voice. He heard it. Clearly.

"Help me!" he called into the bullhorn. "I'll pay you in metal. Okay? Is that okay?" Again he listened. And heard, this time, the scamper of many voices, very shrill, like screams. The noise echoed, blended with the hushed quiver of the weeds.

He got out his binoculars, gazed around him. Nothing but barren countryside, spread out ugly and bleak. Great red spots that hadn't yet been overgrown, and slag surfaces were still visible—but by this time most ruins had become covered by soil and crabgrass. He saw, far off, a robot farming. Plowing with a metal hook welded to its waist, a section torn off some discarded machine. It did not look up; it paid no attention to him because it had never been alive, and only a living thing could care. The robot farmer continued to drag the rusty hook through the hard ground, its pitted body bent double with the strain. Working slowly, silently, without complaint.

And then he saw them. The source of the noise. Twenty of them scampered across the ruined earth toward him; little black boys who leaped and ran, shouting shrill commands back and forth, as if in a single roofless cage.

"Whither, Son of Wrath?" the nearest little boy piped, meanwhile pushing through the tangled debris and slag. He was a little Bantu, in red rags sewn and patched together. He ran up to the cart, like a puppy, leaping and bounding and grinning white-teethed. He broke off bits of green weeds that grew here and there.

"West," Tibor answered. "Always west. But I am stuck here."

The other children sprinted up, now; they formed a circle around the stranded cart. An unusually wild bunch, completely undisciplined. They rolled and fought and tumbled and chased one another madly.

"How many of you," Tibor said, "have taken your first instruction?"

There was a sudden uneasy silence. The children looked at one another guiltily; none of them answered.

"None of you?" Tibor said, amazed. Only thirty miles from Charlottesville. God, he thought; we have broken down like a rusty machine. "How do you expect to phase yourselves with the cosmic will? How can you expect to know the divine plan?" He whipped his grippers toward one of the boys, the nearest to his cart. "Are you constantly preparing yourself for the life to come? Are you constantly purging and purifying yourself? Do you deny yourself meat, sex, entertainment, financial gain, education, leisure?" But it was obvious; their unrestrained laughter and play proved. "Butterflies," he said scathingly, snorting with disgust. "Anyhow," he grated, "get me loose so I can roll on. I order you to!"

The children gathered at the rear of the cart and began to push. The cart bumped against the first fallen tree, going no farther.

"Get in front," Tibor said, "and lift it up. All of you—take hold at the same time!" They did so, obediently but joyfully. He reclutched the cart in forward one—it shuddered and then passed over the first tree, to come to rest halfway up the second. A moment later he found himself bumping over the second tree and up against a third. The cart, raised up, jutting its nose into the sky, whined and groaned, and a wisp of blue smoke trickled up from the engine.

Now he could see better. Farmers, some robot, some alive, worked the fields on all sides. A thin layer of soil over slag; a few limp wheat stalks waved, thin and emaciated. The ground was terrible, the worst he had ever seen. He could feel the metal beneath the cart, almost at the surface. Bent men and women watered their sickly crops with tin cans, old metal containers picked from the ruins. An ox was pulling a crude car.

In another field, women weeded by hand; all moved slowly, stupidly, victims of hookworm from the soil. They were all barefoot. The children evidently hadn't picked it up yet, but they soon would. He gazed up at the clouded sky and gave thanks to the God of Wrath for sparing him this; trials of exceptional vividness lay on every hand. These men and women were being tempered in a hot crucible; their souls were probably purified to an astonishing degree. A baby lay in the shade, beside a half-dozing mother. Flies crept over its eyes; the mother breathed heavily, hoarsely, her mouth open, an unhealthy flush discoloring the paperlike skin. Her belly bulged; she had already become pregnant again. Another eternal soul to be raised from a lower level. Her great breasts sagged and wobbled as she stirred in her sleep, spilling out over her dirty wraparound.

The boys, having pushed him and the Holstein past the logs, the remnants of former trees, trotted off.

"Wait," Tibor said. "Come back. I will ask and you will answer. You know the basic catechisms?" He peered sharply around.

The children returned, eyes on the ground, and assembled in a silent circle around him. One hand went up, then another.

"First," Tibor said. "*Who are you?* You are a minute fragment in the cosmic plan. Second—*what are you?* A mere speck in a system so vast as to be beyond comprehension. Third! *What is the way of life?* To fulfill what is required by the cosmic forces. Fourth! What—"

"Fifth," one of the boys muttered. "*Where have you been?*" He answered his own question. "Through endless steps; each turn of the wheel advances or depresses you."

"Sixth!" Tibor cried. "*What determines your direction at the next turn?* Your conduct in this manifestation.

"Seventh! *What is right conduct?* Submitting yourself to the eternal forces of the Deus Irae, that which makes up the divine plan.

"Eighth! *What is the significance of suffering?* To purify the soul.

"Ninth! *What is the significance of death?* To release the person from this manifestation, so he may rise to a new rung of the ladder.

"Tenth—" But at that moment Tibor broke off. An adult human shape approached his cart; instinctively, his Holstein lowered her head and pretended—or tried—to crop the bitter weeds growing around her.

"We got to go," the black children piped. "Goodbye." They scampered off; one paused, looked back at Tibor, and shouted, "Don't talk to her! My momma say never to talk to her or you get sucked in. Watch out, y'hear?"

"I hear," Tibor said, and shivered. The air had become dark and cool, as if awaiting the thrashing fury of a storm. He knew what this was; he recognized her.

He would go down the ruined streets, toward the sprawling mass of stone and columns that was its house. It had been described to him many times. Each stone was carefully listed on the big map back at Charlottesville. He knew by heart the street that led there, to the entrance. He knew how the great doors lay on their faces, broken and split. He knew how the dark, empty corridors would look inside. He would pass into the vast chamber, the dark room of bats and spiders and echoing sounds. And there it would be. The Great C. Waiting silently, waiting to hear the questions. The queries on which it thrived.

"Who is there?" the shape asked him, the female shape of the Great C's peripatetic extension. The voice sounded again, a metallic voice, hard and penetrating, without warmth in it. An enormous voice that could not be stopped; it would never become still.

He was afraid, more afraid than ever before in his life. His body had begun to shake terribly. Awkwardly he thrashed about in his seat, squinting in the gloom to make out her features. He could not. She had a dished-in face, with almost vestigial features, almost without the courtesy of features at all. That chilled him, too.

"I've—" He swallowed noisily, revealing his fear. "I have come to pay my respects, Great C," he breathed.

"You have prepared questions for me?"

"Yes," he said, lying. He had hoped to sneak past the Great C, not disturbing it, not being disturbed by it either.

"You will ask me within the structure," she said, putting her hand on the railing of his car. "Not out here."

Tibor said, "I do not have to go into the structure. You can answer the questions here." Huskily he cleared his throat, swallowed, pondered the first question; he had carried them with him, in written form, just in case. Thank god he had; thank god that Father Handy had prepared him. She would eventually drag him inside, but he intended to hold off as long as possible. "How did you come into existence?" he asked.

"Is that the first question?"

"No," he said quickly; it certainly was not.

"I don't recognize you," the mobile extension of the giant computer said, her voice tinny and shrill. "Are you from another area?"

"Charlottesville," Tibor said.

"And you came this way to question me?"

"Yes," he lied. He reached into his coat pocket; one of his manual extensors checked that the derringer .22 pistol, single shot, which Father Handy had given him, was still there. "I have a gun," he said.

"Do you?" Her tone was scathing, in an abstract sort of way.

"I've never fired a pistol before," Tibor said. "We have bullets, but I don't know if they still work."

"What is your name?"

"Tibor McMasters. I'm an incomplete; I have no arms or legs."

"A phocomelus," the Great C said.

"Pardon?" he said, half stammering.

"You are a young man," she said. "I can see you fairly well. Part of my equipment was destroyed in the Smash, but I can still see a little. Originally, I scanned mathematical questions visually. It saved time. I see you have military clothing. Where did you get it? Your tribe does not make such things, does it?"

"No, this is military garb. United Nations, by the color, I would say." Tremblingly, he rasped, "Is it true that you come originally from the hand of the God of Wrath? That he manufactured you in order to put the world to fire? Made suddenly terrible—by atoms. And that you invented the atoms and delivered them to the world, corrupting God's original plan? We know you did it," he finished. "But we don't know how."

"That is your first question? I will never tell you. It is too terrible for you ever to know. Lufteufel was insane; he made me do insane things."

"Men other than the Deus Irae came to visit you," Tibor said. "They came and listened."

"You know," the Great C said, "I have existed a long time. I remember life before the Smash. I could tell you many things about it. Life was much different then. You wear a beard and hunt animals in the woods. Before the Smash there were no woods. Only cities and farms. And men were clean-shaven. Many of them wore white clothing, then. They were scientists. They were very fine. I was constructed by engineers; they were a form of scientist." She paused. "Do you recognize the name Einstein? Albert Einstein?"

"No."

"He was the greatest scientist of them all, but he never consulted me because he was already dead when I was made. There were even questions I could answer which even he failed to ask. There were other computers, but none so grand as I. Everyone alive now has heard of me, have they not?"

"Yes," Tibor said, and wondered how and when he was going to get away; it, she, had him trapped here. Wasting his time with its obligatory mumbling.

"What is your first question?" the Great C asked.

Fear surged up within him. "Let me see," he said. "I have to word it exactly right."

"You're goddamn right you have to," the Great C said, in its emotionless voice.

Huskily, with a dry throat, Tibor said, "I'll give you the easiest one first." With his right manual extensor he grappled the slip within his coat pocket, brought it forth, and held it in front of his eyes. Taking a deep, unsteady breath, he said, "Where does the rain come from?"

There was silence.

"Do you know?" he asked, waiting tensely.

"Rain comes originally from the earth, mostly from

the oceans. It rises into the air by a process called 'evaporation.' The agent of the process is the heat of the sun. The moisture of the oceans ascends in the form of minute particles. These particles, when they are high enough, enter a colder band of air. At this point, condensation occurs. The moisture collects into what are called great clouds. When a sufficient amount is collected, the water descends again in drops. You call the drops rain."

Tibor plucked at his chin with his left manual extensor and said, "Hmmm. I see. You're *sure?*" It did sound familiar; possibly, in a better age, he had learned it some time ago.

"Next question," the Great C said.

"This is more difficult," Tibor said huskily. The Great C had answered about rain, but surely it could not know the answer to this question. "Tell me," he said slowly, "if you can: What keeps the sun moving through the sky? Why doesn't it fall to the ground?"

The mobile extension of the computer gave an odd whirr, almost a laugh. "You will be astonished by the answer. The sun does not move. At least, what you see as motion is not motion at all. What you see is the motion of the Earth as it revolves around the sun. Since you are standing still, it seems as if the sun is moving, but that is not so; all the nine planets, including the Earth, revolve about the sun in regular elliptical orbits. They have been doing so for several billion years. Does that answer your question?"

Tibor's heart constricted. At last he managed to pull himself together, but he could not shake the pulsing prickles of cold-heat that had gathered on his body. "Christ," he snarled, half to himself, half at the near-featureless female figure standing by his cart. "Well, for what it's worth, I'll ask you the last of my three questions." But it would know the answer, as it had the initial two. "You can't possibly answer this. No living creature could know. How did the world begin? You see, you did not exist before the world. Therefore it is impossible that you could know."

"There are several theories," the Great C said calmly. "The most satisfactory is the nebular hypothesis. According to this—"

"No hypothesis," Tibor said.

"But—"

"I want facts," Tibor said.

Time passed. Neither of them spoke. Then, at last, the blurred female figure palpitated into her imitation of life. "Take the lunar fragments obtained in 1969. They show an age of—"

"Inferences," Tibor said.

"The universe is at least five billion—"

"No," Tibor said. "You don't know. You don't remember. The part of you that contained the answer got destroyed in the Smash." He laughed with what he hoped was a confident sound . . . but, as it came it wriggled with insecurity; his voice drained off into near silence. "You are senile," he said, virtually inaudibly. "Like an old man damaged by radiation; you're just a hollow chitinous shell." He did not know what "chitinous" meant, but the term was a favorite of Father Handy; hence, he used it now.

At this crucial moment the Great C vacillated. It's not sure, he said to himself, if it answered the question. Doubt edged its voice as it quavered, "Come subsurface with me and show me the damaged or missing memory tape."

"How can I show you a missing tape?" Tibor said, and laughed loudly, a barking woof that spilled out searingly.

"I guess you're right, there," the Great C muttered; now the female figure hesitated, drew back from his car and cow. "I want to feed on you," it said. "Come below so I can dissolve you, as I have the others, the ones who came this way before you."

"No," Tibor said. He sent his manual grapples into the inside pocket of his coat, brought forth the derringer, aimed it at the control unit, the brain, of the mobile extension confronting him. "Bang," he said, and again laughed. "You're dead."

"No such thing," the Great C said. Its voice seemed more hardy, now. "How would you like to be my caretaker? If we go below you'll see—"

Tibor fired the single shot; the projectile bounced off the metal head unit of the mobile extension and disappeared. The figure closed its eyes, opened them, studied Tibor lengthily. It then glanced around doubtfully, as if unsure what it should do; it blinked and by degrees collapsed, lying at last among the weeds.

Tibor gathered his four extensions above it, took hold, and lifted—or rather tried to lift. The object, folded up now, like a chair, did not move. The hell with it; there's no value in it anyhow, even if I could lift it, he decided. And the damn cow couldn't possibly pull such a massive and inert load.

He flicked at the rump of the cow, delivering a signal to it; the cow lumbered forward, dragging his cart after it.

I got away, he said to himself. The horde of black children ebbed back, making a way open to him; they had watched the entire interaction between himself and the Great C. Why doesn't it dissolve them? Tibor wondered. Strange.

The cow reached the road beyond the felled trees and continued slowly on its way. Flies buzzed at it but the cow ignored them, as if the cow, too, understood the dignity of triumph.

EIGHT

Higher and higher the cow climbed; she passed through a deep rift between two rocky ridges. Huge roots from old stumps spurted out on all sides. The cow followed a dried-up creekbed, winding and turning.

After a time, mists began to blow about Tibor. The cow paused at the top of the ridge, breathing deeply, looking back the way they had come.

A few drops of poisoned rain stirred the leaves around them. Again the wind moved through the great dead trees along the ridge. Tibor flicked at the cow rump ahead of him, and the cow once more shuddered into motion.

He was, all at once, on a rocky field, overgrown with plantain and dandelion, infested with the dry stalks of yesterday's weeds. They came to a ruined fence, broken and rotting. Was he going the right way? Tibor got out one of his Richfield maps, studied it, held it before his eyes like an Oriental scroll. Yes; this was the right way; he would encounter the tribes of the south, and from there—

The cow dragged the cart through the fence, and arrived at last before a tumbledown well, half filled with stones and earth. Tibor's heart beat quickly, fluttering with nervous excitement. What lay ahead? The remains of a building, sagging timbers and broken glass, a few ruined pieces of furniture strewn nearby. An old automobile tire caked and cracked. Some damp rags heaped over the rusty, bent bedroom springs. Along the edge of the field there was a grove of ancient trees. Lifeless trees, withered and inert, their thin, blackened stalks rising up leaflessly. Broken sticks stuck in the hard ground. Row after row of dead trees, some bent and leaning, torn loose from the rocky soil by the unending wind.

Tibor had the cow move across the field to the orchard of dead trees. The wind surged against him without respite, whipping the foul-smelling mists into his nostrils and face. His skin was damp and shiny with the mist. He coughed and urged the cow on; it stumbled on, over the rocks and clods of earth, trembling.

"Hold," Tibor said, reining the cow to a stop.

For a long time he gazed at the withered old apple tree. He could not take his eyes from it. The sight of the ancient tree—the only living one in the orchard—fascinated and repelled him. The only one alive, he thought. The other trees had lost the struggle . . . but this tree still clung to precarious semilife.

The tree looked hard and barren. Only a few dark leaves hung from it—and some withered apples, dried and seasoned by the wind and mists. They had stayed there, on the branches, forgotten and abandoned. The ground around the trees seemed cracked and bleak. Stones and decayed heaps of older leaves in ragged clumps.

Extending his front right extensor, Tibor plucked a leaf from the tree and examined it.

What have I got here? he wondered.

The tree swayed ominously. Its gnarled branches rubbed together. Something in the sound made Tibor pull back.

Night was coming. The sky had darkened radically. A burst of frigid wind struck him, half turning him around in his seat. Tibor shuddered, bracing himself against it, pulling his log coat around him. Below, the floor of the valley was disappearing into shadow, into the vast nod of night.

In the darkening mists the tree seemed stern and menacing. A few leaves blew from it, drifting and swirling with the wind. A leaf blew past Tibor's head; he tried to grasp it, but it escaped and disappeared. He felt all at once terribly tired, as well as frightened. I'm getting out of here, he said to himself, and nudged the cow into motion.

And then he saw the apple, and it all was different immediately.

Tibor activated the battery-powered radio mounted behind him in the car. "Father," he said. "I can't go on." He waited, but the receiving portion of the two-way radio sent forth only the rushing noise of static. No voices. For a moment he tuned the receiver's dial, hoping to pick up someone somewhere. Tibor the unlucky, he thought. A world, a whole world of sorrow—I have to carry it, that which can't be carried. And within me my heart breaks.

You wanted it like this, he thought. You wanted to be happy, unendingly happy . . . or find unending grief. And this way you achieved endless grief. Lost here at sundown, at least thirty miles from home. Where are you going now? he wondered.

Pressing the button of his microphone, he grated, "Father Handy, I can't stand it. There is nothing out here except what's dead; it's all dead. You read me?" He listened to the radio, tuning it on to Father Handy's beam. Static. No voice.

In the gloom, the apple from the apple tree glistened moistly. It looked black, now, but it was of course only red. Probably rotten, he thought. Not worth eating. And yet it wants me to eat.

Maybe it's a magic tree, he said to himself. I've never before seen one, but Father Handy tells about them. And if I eat the apple, something good will happen. The Christians—Father Abernathy—would say the apple is evil, a product of Satan, and that if you bite into it you sin. But we don't believe that, he said to himself. Anyhow that was long ago and in another land. And he had not eaten all day; he had become famished.

I'll pick it up, he decided. But I won't eat it.

He sent a manual extensor after the apple, and, a moment later, held it directly before his eyes, a beam from his miner's hat illuminating it. And somehow it seemed important. But—

Something stirred at the periphery of his vision; he glanced swiftly up.

"Good evening," the leaner of the two shapes said. "You are not from here, are you?" The two shapes came up to the car and stood bathed in light. Two young males, tall and thin and horny blue-gray like ashes. The one who had spoken raised his hand in greeting. Six of seven fingers—and extra joints.

"Hello," Tibor said. One had an ax, a foliage ax. The other carried only his pants and the remains of a canvas shirt. They were nearly eight feet tall. No flesh—bones and hard angles and large, curious eyes, heavily lidded. There undoubtedly were internal changes, radically different metabolism and cell structure, ability to utilize hot salts, altered digestive system. They both stared at Tibor with interest.

"Say," one of them said. "'You're a human being.'"

"That's right," Tibor said.

"My name's Jackson." The youth extended his thin blue horny hand and Tibor shook it awkwardly with his front right extensor. "My friend here is Earl Potter."

Tibor shook hands with Potter. "Greetings," Potter said. His scaly rough lips twitched. "Can we have a look at your rig, that cart you're tied into? We've never seen anything quite like it."

Muties, Tibor said to himself. The lizard kind. He managed to suppress a thrill of aversion; he made his face smile. "I'm willing to let you look at what I have," he said. "But I can't leave the cart; I don't have any arms or legs, just these grippers."

"Yeah," Jackson said, nodding. "So we see." He slapped the cow on its flank; the cow mooed and raised her head. Her tail, in the evening gloom, switched from side to side. "How fast can she pull you?" he asked Tibor.

"Fast enough." In his front left gripper he held his single-shot pistol; if they tried to kill him he would get one of them. But not both. "I'm based about thirty miles from here," he said. "In what we call Charlottesville. Have you heard of us?"

"Sure," Jackson said. "How many are there of you?"

Tibor said cautiously, "One hundred and five." He exaggerated, deliberately; the larger the camp, the greater the chance that they would not kill him. After all, some of the hundred and five might come looking for revenge.

"How have you survived?" Potter asked. "This whole area was hard hit, wasn't it?"

"We hid in mines," Tibor said. "Our ancestors; they burrowed down deep when the Smash began. We're fairly well set up. Grow our own food in tanks, a few machines, pumps and compressors and electrical generators. Some hand lathes. Looms." He didn't mention that generators now had to be cranked by hand, that only about half of the tanks were still operative. After ninety years metal and plastic weren't much good—despite endless patching and repairing. Everything was wearing out and breaking down.

"Say," Potter said. "This sure makes a fool of Dave Hunter."

"Dave? Big fat Dave?" Jackson said.

Potter said, "Dave says there aren't any true humans left outside this area." He poked at Tibor's helmet curiously. "Our settlement's an hour away by tractor—our hunting tractor. Earl and I were out hunting flap rabbits. Good meat but hard to bring down—weigh about twenty-five pounds."

"What do you use?" Tibor asked. "Not that ax, surely."

Potter and Jackson laughed. "Look at this here." Potter slid a long brass rod from his trousers. It fitted down inside his pants along his pipe-stem leg.

Tibor examined the rod. It was tooled by hand. Soft brass, carefully bored and straightened. One end was shaped into a nozzle. He peered down it. A tiny metal pin was lodged in a cake of transparent material. "How does it work?" he asked.

"Launched by hand," Potter said. "Like a blow gun. But once the b-dart is in the air, it follows its target forever. The initial thrust has to be provided." Potter laughed. "I supply that. A big puff of air."

"Interesting," Tibor said with elaborate casualness. Studying the two blue-gray faces, he asked, "Many humans near here?"

"Damn near none," Potter and Jackson mumbled together. "What do you say about staying with us awhile? The Old Man will be pleased to welcome you; you're the first human we've seen this month. What do you say? We'll take care of you, feed you, bring you cold plants and animals, for a week, maybe?"

"Sorry," Tibor said. "Other business. But if I come through here on my way back . . ." He rummaged in the sack of artifacts and tools next to him. "See this picture?" he said, holding up the dim piece of paper on which was printed a picture—of sorts—of Carleton Lufteufel. "Do you recognize this man?"

Potter and Jackson studied the picture. "A human being," Potter said. "Frankly, you all tend to look alike to us." They handed the picture back to Tibor. "But the Old Man might recognize it," Jackson said. "Come with us; it's lucky to have a human being staying with you. What do you say?"

"No." Tibor shook his head. "I have to keep going; I have to find this man."

Jackson's face fell in disappointment. "Not for a little while? Overnight? We'll pump you plenty of cold food. We have a fine lead-sealed cooler the Old Man fixed up."

"You're sure there're no humans in this region?" Tibor said as he prepared to continue on; he slapped the rump of the cow briskly.

"We thought for a while there weren't any left anywhere. A rumor once in a while. But you're the first we've seen in a couple of years." Potter pointed west. "There's a tribe of rollers off that way." He pointed vaguely south. "A couple of tribes of bugs, too."

"And some runners," Jackson said. "And north there's some kind of underground ones—the blind digging kind." Potter and Jackson both made a face. "I can't see them and their bores and scoops. But what the hell." He grinned. "Everybody has his own way. I guess to you we lizards seem sort of—" He gestured. "Weird."

Tibor said, "What's the story on this apple tree? Is this the tree from which the Christian-Jewish idea of the serpent in the garden of eden comes?"

"It's our understanding that the Garden of Eden is located around a hundred miles to the east," Jackson said. "You're a Christian, are you?" Tibor nodded. "And that picture you showed us—

"A Christian deity," Jackson said.

"No." Tibor shook his head firmly. Amazing, he thought; they don't seem to know anything about the SOWs or about us. Well, he thought, we didn't know much about *them*.

A third lizard approached. "Greetings, natural," it said, holding its open palm up in the air. "I just wanted to get a look at a human being." It studied Tibor. "You're not all that different. Can you live on the surface?"

"Pretty well," Tibor said. "But I'm not exactly a human; I'm what we called an inc—incomplete. As you can see." He showed the third lizard the photo of Carleton Lufteufel. "Have you ever seen this man? Think. It's important to me."

"You're trying to find him?" the third lizard said. "Yes, it's obvious that you are on a Pilg; why else would you be traveling, especially at night, and with you handicapped by virtue of the fact that you don't have any legs or feet and no arms. That's a smart car you've built yourself. But *how* did you do it, lacking hands? Did someone else build it for you? And if they did, why? Are you valuable?"

"I'm a painter," Tibor said simply.

"Then you're valuable," the lizard said. "Listen, inc. Did you know that someone's following you?"

"What?" Tibor said, instantly tense and alert. "Who?" he demanded.

"Another actual human," the lizard said. "But on a machine with two big wheels, propelled by a chain-linked gear system, pedally operated. A bykel, I think it's called."

"Bicycle," Tibor said.

"Yes, exactly."

"Can you hide me?" Tibor asked, and then thought,

They're making it up; they just want to get me into their settlement where they can absorb some of my luck.

"Sure we can hide you," all three lizards said simultaneously.

"On the other hand," Tibor said, "a human would not kill another human." But he knew it was untrue; plenty of humans killed and injured other humans; after all, the giant Smash had been brought on by humans.

The three lizards huddled, conferring. Then, abruptly, they stood up, turned to face Tibor. "Do you have any metal money?" Jackson asked, in a kind of deliberately careless, offhand way.

"None," Tibor said cautiously. This also was untrue; he had an alloy fifty-cent piece in a secret crevasse of his car.

"I ask that," Jackson said, "because we have a dog we would be willing to sell you."

"A what? Tibor said.

"Dog." Potter and Jackson trooped off, disappearing into the darkness; evidently their vision was enormously improved over human standards.

"Have you never seen a dog?" the remaining lizard asked.

"Yes, but it was a long time ago," Tibor answered, lying again.

The lizard said, "A dog, your dog, would drive off the other human—that is, if you gave him the proper command. They have to be trained, of course; they're lower on the evolutionary scale as compared to humans and we alike. They're not like those double-domed dogs people bred before the Smash."

Tibor said, "Would a dog be able to find the man I am looking for?"

"What man?"

Tibor showed it the blotched photograph of Carleton Lufteufel.

"You want him?" the lizard said, studying the face. "Is he a neat guy?"

"I can't say," Tibor said obliquely.

The lizard handed him back the photograph. "Is there a reward?"

Tibor pondered. "A fifty-cent piece," he said.

"Really?" The lizard fluffed up his scales excitedly. "Payable dead or alive?"

"He can't die," Tibor said.

"Everyone dies."

"He will not die."

"Is he—supernatural?"

"Yes." Tibor nodded.

"I have never seen a supernatural," the lizard declared; he shook his head firmly. "Not in my entire life."

"You have a religion, do you?"

"Yes. We worship the dawn."

"Quaint," Tibor said.

"When the sun comes," the lizard said, "evil vanishes from the world. Do you believe there's life on the sun?"

"It's too hot," Tibor said.

"But they could be made out of diamonds."

Tibor said, "Nothing can live on the sun."

"How fast does the sun move?"

"About a million miles per hour."

"It's bigger than it looks, isn't it?" The lizard peered at him.

"Much bigger. Almost a billion miles in circumference."

"Have you been there?" the lizard asked.

"I said," Tibor said, "No life can exist on the sun. Anyhow, the surface is melted; there wouldn't be any place to stand." Who is it following me? he wondered. "A highwayman?" he asked aloud. "The human lurking me—what's he look like?"

"Young," the lizard said.

"Pete Sands," Tibor said flatly.

The two other lizards emerged from the darkness; Potter held a great gray animal who whined passionately when it saw Tibor—a whine of love. Tibor studied it; the dog studied him in return.

"Toby likes you," Jackson said.

"I would like a dog very much," Tibor said yearningly. It would be his friend, the way Tom Swift And His Electric Magic Carpet was to Pete. A deep and strange feeling welled up in him, a hope. "Wow," he said. He sent his front extensors out to grapple gently at the quivering brown mop of fur, the glorious tail wagger. "But are you willing to part with such a fine—"

Jackson said brusquely, "Humans must be protected. It is the law. We knew this from the moment of our births."

"So they can repopulate back," Potter said. "With their intact genes."

"What's a gene?" Tibor asked.

Potter gestured. "You know. An ingredient in masculine sperm."

"What's sperm?" Tibor asked.

They all laughed, but, shyly, did not answer.

"What does this dog eat?" Tibor asked, then.

"Anything," Jackson said. "He can forage. He is reliant."

"How long will he live?"

"Oh, probably two to three hundred years."

Tibor said, "Then he will outlive me." For some reason this depressed him; all at once he felt weak and cold. I shouldn't feel this way, he reasoned with himself. Already brought down by thoughts of separation. After all, I'm a human being. At least these lizards think I am; I'm good enough for them. I should feel strength

and pride, he thought, and not envision ahead already
that terrible end of friendships, for us all.

Suddenly the three lizards whipped about, peering
into the darkness, their bodies straining against or toward something invisible.

"What is it?" Tibor said; again he clutched at the pistol concealed on his person.

"Bugs," Potter said laconically.

"The dumb bastards," Jackson said.

Bugs, Tibor thought. How horrible. He had heard of
them many times, them and their multifaceted eyes,
their gleaming shells—a weird conglomeration of unhu-
man parts. And to think that they bred their way out of
mammals, he thought, and in such a few short years.
Speeded up frantically by the radiation. We're related to
them and they stink. They offend the world. And surely
they offend God.

"What are you doing there?" a metallic voice buzzed.
Tibor saw them moving, upright; they lurched toward
the light. "Lizzys," the bug said scathingly. "And—
Frebis forbid!—an inc."

Five bugs stood by the light now, warming their—
Christ, Tibor thought. Warming their brittle bodies; if a
bug was hit directly in the breadbasket, it broke in half.
So much for bugs: they depended mainly on their facile
tongues to get them what they wanted. Bugs talked their
way out of a good deal of trouble; they were the lie-
spinners of Earth.

These were unarmed. As near as he could make out.
And, standing by his cart, the three lizards relaxed;
their fear had departed.

"Hey, bug," Jackson said, nodding toward one of the
chitin-shelled creatures. "How come you have lungs?
Where'd you get them? Vermin shouldn't have lungs.
It's against nature."

Potter said, "We ought to cook us up a little bug soup."

Incredulous, Tibor said, "You mean you *eat* them?"

"Right," the third lizard said, his arms folded, leaning against Tibor's cart. "When times are tough . . . they taste awful."

"You rotting obnoxious freak," one bug said. They did not seem frightened; they made no move in the direction of escape.

"Does your tail come off?" another bug said to the three lizards.

"What tail?" another bug said. "That's its pecker hanging down behind it. Lizards' peckers stick out behind, not in front."

The bugs laughed coarsely.

"I saw this lizard once," a bug declared, "who had an erection—and he got scared off, I guess her husband came back, and he tried to run, and all the husband had to do was tromp down with his foot on that great hard pecker sticking out behind." All the bugs laughed; they seemed to be enjoying themselves.

"What happened after he tromped down on it?" a bug asked. "Did it come off then?"

"It came off," the other bug continued, "and it lay there twitching and flopping in the dirt until sundown."

Potter said, "Let's take these insects down a peg or two. Listen to them—they're uppity." He glanced around him, apparently seeking something to use as a weapon. He took his time and the bugs did not move; they seemed relaxed and confident.

And now Tibor saw why. The bugs had not ventured out alone. A score of runners had accompanied them.

NINE

This was not his first encounter with runners. Back in Charlottesville, runners came and went unmolested. Wherever runners could be found, a kind of peace prevailed, an idiomatic tranquility, engendered by the benign habits of the runners themselves.

The good-natured little faces peered up at Tibor. The creatures were not over four feet high. Fat and round, covered with thick pelts . . . beady eyes, quivering noses—and great kangaroo legs.

Amazing, these swift evolutionary entelechies, cast forth from what were essentially poisons. So many and so fast; so many immediate kinds. Nature, striving to overcome the filth of the war: the toxins.

"Clearness be with you," the runners said, virtually in unison. Their whiskers twitched. "How come you don't have any arms or legs? You're very strange as a life-form."

"The war," Tibor said vaguely, resenting the pushiness of the runners.

"Did you know your cart is malfunctioning?" the runners asked.

"No," he said, taken by surprise. "Doesn't it run? It got me this far; I mean—" Panic flew up inside him.

"There is an autofac near here that still works a little," the largest of the runners said. "It can't do very much—not like it could in olden times. But it could probably replace the wheel bearings in your cart that are running dry. And the cost is not all that great."

"Oh yes," Tibor said. "The wheel bearings. They probably are running dry." He lifted one wheel off the ground and spun it noisily. "You're right," he admitted. "Where's the autofac?"

"A few miles north of here," the smallest of the runners said. "Follow me." The other runners scampered into a group that eased itself off. "Or rather," the runner amended, "follow us. Hey, are you guys coming along, too?"

"Sure," the body of runners said, whiskers twitching. They obviously did not want to miss out on any of the action.

To Potter and Jackson, Tibor said, "Can I trust them?" He held in his mind, at this moment, a nebulous fear: Suppose the runners led him off to some desolate region, then killed him and stole his cart? It seemed a distinct possibility, the times being what they were.

Potter said, "You can trust them. They're harmless. Which is more than you can say for these damn bugs." He kicked at a cluster of bugs; they scuttled away, avoiding his scaly foot.

"An autofac, an autofac," the runners chanted happily as they raced off. Tibor cautiously followed. "We're going to the autofac and get the limbless man a cheap repair. It's guaranteed for a thousand years or a million miles; whichever comes first." Giggling to themselves, the runners disappeared for a moment, then reappeared, beckoning Tibor genially on.

"Catch you coming back," Jackson yelled after Tibor. "Make sure you get a written guarantee, just to be safe."

"You mean," Tibor said, "that I can expect tarrididdle from an autofac?" It must be a Russian one, he thought. The Russian autofacs were Byzantine in their

convolutions of intellect. They seemed for the most part
to be excellently built, however. If this one still func-
tioned at all, it could undoubtedly repair his dry-
running wheel bearings.

He wondered how much it would charge.

They reached the autofac at dawn. Brilliantly colored
clouds, like the fingerpaintings of a baby, stretched
across the sky. Birds or quasi-birds chirped in the
weedy bushes growing on all sides of the runners' fire-
path.

"It's around here somewhere," Earl, the leader of the
runners, said as he halted; his name, stitched in red
thread on the bosom of his worksuit, declared itself to
Tibor. "Wait; let me think." He pondered at length.

"How about a bite to eat?" a runner asked Earl.

"We can get something from the autofac," Earl said,
nodding his shaggy head wisely. "Come on, inc." He
jerked an abrupt arm motion at Tibor. During the night,
the click-clacking of the dry wheel bearings had become
hideously loud; the assembly would not function much
longer. "We make a right turn here," Earl said, advancing toward a yarrow thicket, "then a sharp left." Only
his tail could be seen as he struggled into the stiff brush
of the thicket. "Here's the entrance!" he called presently, and waved Tibor to follow him.

"Will it cost very much?" Tibor said apprehensively.

"Won't cost," Earl said, thrashing about in the shrubbery a short distance ahead of Tibor. "Nobody comes
this way anymore; it's perishing. It'll be glad to see us.
These things, they have emotions, too. Of sorts."

An opening appeared ahead of Tibor as he floun-
dered about in his unwieldy cart. A weedless place, as
free of grass as if it had been shaved. In the center of
the open place he could make out a flat, large disc, evidently metal; clamped shut, it greeted him soundlessly,

confronting him with its meaningful presence. Yes, he thought, it's a Russian autofac that landed here in seed form from an orbiting satellite. Probably in the last days of the war, during which the enemy tried everything.

"Hi," he said to the autofac.

A shiver passed through the runners. "Don't talk to it like that," Earl said, nervously. "Have more respect; this thing can kill us all."

"Greetings," Tibor said.

"If you're pompous or boorish," Earl said quietly, "it'll kill us." His tone was patient. As if, Tibor thought, he's addressing a child. And perhaps that is what I am, vis-à-vis this construct: a baby who knows no better. This thing, after all, is no natural mutant. It was *made*.

"My friend," Tibor said to the autofac. "Can you help me?"

Earl groaned.

"You call it, then," Tibor said to him, feeling irritated. How many verbal rituals had to surround the summoning of the intelligence of this wartime human construct? Evidently a very large number. "Look," he said to Earl, and also to the autofac, "I need its help but I'm not going to fall in a groveling heap and pray it to install new wheel bearings in my cart. It's not worth it." The hell with it, he thought. These are the entities which brought our race down; these did us in.

"Mighty autofac," Earl said sonorously. "We pray for your good assistance. This wretched armless/legless man cannot complete his journey without your beneficent assistance. Could you take a moment to examine his vehicle? The right front wheel bearings have failed him in his hour of need." He paused, listening intently, his doglike head cocked.

"Here it comes," the smallest of the runners said in a rapt, appreciative tone of voice; he seemed awed.

The lid of the autofac slid back. A lift from beneath

the entrance thrust up a tall metal stalk, on the end of which a bullhorn could be seen. The bullhorn swiveled, then lined itself up so that it directly faced Tibor.

"You are pregnant, are you?" the bullhorn brayed. "I can supply you with ancient cures: arsenic, iron rust, water in which the dead have been immersed, mule's kidneys, the froth from the mouth of a camel—which do you prefer?"

"No," Earl said. "He's not pregnant. He has a wheel bearing that's running dry. Try to pay attention, sir."

"I'll not be talked to like that," the autofac said. A second rod jutted up, now. It appeared to have a gas nozzle mounted at ground level. "You must die," the autofac said, and emitted several meager puffs of gray smoke. The runners retreated. "I require great amounts of freczibble . . ." The dour sounds emitted by the autofac faded into an indistinct mass of noise; something in the speech circuit had failed to function. The two vertical rods whipped back and forth in agitation, emitted a little more gas, harmlessly, then became inert. A curl of black smoke ascended from the entranceway of the autofac, then a whine. Of gear teeth, Tibor decided.

To Earl, Tibor said, "Why is it so hostile?"

Immediately coarse clouds of black issued forth from the underground reality which was the autofac. "I'm not hostile!" the bullhorn honked with wrath. "You goddamn lying son of a bitch." A hiss, like steam released in an emergency overload, and then a huge crashing roar, as if a tone of garbage-can lids had been upset by raccoons. Then—silence.

"I think you killed it," the smallest of the runners said to Earl.

"Christ," Earl said, with disgust. "Well, it probably couldn't have helped you anyhow." His voice quavered, then. "It would appear that I have screwed everything up. I wonder what we do now."

Tibor said, "I'll continue on my way." He flicked the cow with a manual extensor; the cow mooed, grunted, and slowly resumed its march, back in the direction from which they had come.

"Wait," Earl said, raising a furred hand. "Let's try once more." He searched in his tunic, and brought forth a notepad and a ballpoint pen of prewar vintage. "We'll submit our request in writing, like they used to do. We'll just drop it down into the hole. And if that don't work, we'll give up." He painfully, slowly scribbled on the notepad, then tore the top page off, and walked slowly toward the inert entrance to the subsurface autofac.

"Once warned twice burned," the smallest of the runners piped.

"Forget it," Tibor said to the runners; again he nudged the cow electronically, and he and she moved off, groaningly, the dry wheel bearings of his cart clacking noisily.

"The trouble may have existed in the bullhorn," Earl said, still trying to knit the situation together. "If we bypass that—"

"Goodbye," Tibor said, and continued on.

He felt melancholy. A soothing sort, a kind of inner peace. Had the runners managed that? He wondered. They were said to . . . the big runner Earl had radiated anything but peace, however. Very strange, he thought; the runners are like the calm eye of the storm that everyone talks about but which no one sees. Peace in the center of chaos, perhaps.

As his cart lumbered on, pulled by his tireless cow, Tibor began to sing.

Brighten up the corner where you are . . .

He could not remember how the rest of the old hymn went, so he tried another.

> This is my father's world. The
> rocks and trees, the wind and
> breeze . . .

That didn't sound right. So he tried the Old One Hundred, the doxology:

> Praise him from whom all blessings
> flow. Praise him ye creatures here
> below. Praise him above, ye heavenly
> host. Thank Father, Son and Holy Ghost.

Or however it was that the hymn went.

He felt better, now. And then all at once he realized that his wheel bearing had stopped complaining. He peered down, and saw the grim news: the wheel had entirely stopped turning. The bearings had seized up.

Well, thus it goes, he thought as he reined the cow to a halt. This is as far as we go, you and I. He sat listening to the sounds around him, noises from the trees and shrubbery, little animals at work, even smaller ones at play: the offspring of the world, maimed and grotesque as they might be, had the right to frolic about in the warm morning sun. The owls had retired; now came the red-tailed hawks. He heard a far-off bird, and was comforted.

The bird sang words, now. *Brighten up the corner*, it called. Again it sang the few words, and then trilled out, *Praise him from whom the wing and trees, the rocks and thank you.* Tweet, toodle. It started from the beginning again, tracing each previous outburst.

A meta-mutant bird, he realized. A *teilhard de chardin:* forward oddity. Does it understand what it sings? he wondered. Or is it like a parrot? He could not tell. He could not go that way; he could only sit. Damn that wheel bearing, he said savagely to himself. If I could converse with the meta-bird maybe I could learn something. Maybe it has seen the Deus Irae and would know where he is.

Something at his right lashed the bushes, something large. And now he saw—saw and did not believe.

A huge worm had begun to uncurl and move toward him. It thrust the bushes aside; it dragged itself on its own oily slime, and as it came toward him it began to scream, high-pitched, strident. Not knowing what to do, he sat frozen, waiting. The rivulets of slime splashed over tarnished gray and brown and green leaves, withering both them and their branches. Dead fruit fell from the rotting trees; there arose a cloud of dry soil particles as the worm snorted and swung its way toward him. "Hi there!" the worm shrieked. It had almost reached him. "I can kill you!" the worm declared, tossing spit and dust and slime in his direction. "Get away and leave me! I guard something very precious, something you want but cannot have. Do you understand? Do you hear me?"

Tibor said, "I can't leave." His voice shook; with his trembling body he engineered a quick movement; he brought forth his derringer once more and aimed it at the cranium of the worm.

"I came out of garbage!" the worm cried. "I was spawned by the wastes of the field! I came from your war, inc. It is your fault that I am ugly like this. You can see the ugliness about me—look." Its straining head wove and bobbed above Tibor's, and now a shower of slime and spit rained down on him. He shut his eyes and shuddered. "Look at me!" the worm shouted.

"Black worm," Tibor grated; he fooled with the derringer, aimlessly. And squinched down to avoid what had to come. It would bite his head off; he would die.

He shut his eyes, and felt the forked tongue of it lap at him.

"I am poisoning you," the worm declared shrilly. "Sniff the odor of my great eternal body. I can never die; I am the Urworm, and I will exist until the end of the Earth!" Coils of its body splashed forward, spilling over his cart, over the cow, over himself. He snapped on the electric field of his cart, a last-ditch, hopeless effort to protect himself and the cow. The field hummed and buzzed; it crackled with shimmering sparks, and, all at once, the head portion of the worm retreated.

"Did I get you?" Tibor said, with hope. "Can't you endure a five-amp electrical charge?" He snapped the dial to peak power; now the field sparked wildly, sending out cascading handfuls of light.

The head of the worm drew far back, to strike. This is it, Tibor realized, and held up the derringer. The head slithered forward and the great beak of the thing crashed through the five-amp field at Tibor.

As it revealed its fangs the electrical field made it pause; it halted its forward motion. Looking up, Tibor saw the soft underside of its throat, and he fired the derringer.

"I want to sleep!" the worm howled. "Why do you disturb my rest?" It jerked back its head, lifted it high, saw the blood dripping down onto itself. "What have you done?" it demanded. It swooped at him once again. He reloaded the derringer, not looking up until he had swung the barrel back into place.

Once more the head descended. Once more he saw up at the soft underside of its throat. Again he fired.

"Let me be!" the worm cried out in pain. "Leave me to my sleep upon my possessions!" It reared up, and then, with a tremendous crash, descended to strike the ground. Its heaping coils spread out everywhere; the worm breathed hoarsely, its glazed eyes fixed on Tibor. "What has been done to you," the worm snarled, "that has caused you to murder me? Have I done any act against you, any crime?"

"No," Tibor said. "None." He could see that it had been badly hurt, and his heart stopped laboring. Again he could breathe. "I am sorry," he said insincerely. "One of the two of us had to—" He paused to reload the derringer. "Only one of us could live," he said, and this time shot the worm between its lidded eyes. The eyes grow and contract, he noticed. Bigger, brighter . . . then paling out to mere glimmers. Mere decay. "You are dead," he said.

The worm did not answer. Its eyes still open, it had died.

Tibor reached with a manual extensor; he dipped his "hand" in the oily slime of the worm, an idea coming to his head. If the slime was truly oily, perhaps he could soak the wheel bearings with it, give them a shield of lubrication. But then something that the worm had said popped up within his mind, an interesting point. The worm had said, "Leave me to my sleep upon my possessions." What did it possess?

He cautiously navigated his cart around the side of the dead worm, prodding the cow expertly with his pseudowhips.

Beyond the tangle of shrubbery—a cave in the side of a rocky hill. It reeked of the worm slime; Tibor got out a handkerchief and held it before his nose, trying to reduce the smell. He then snapped on his light, shone it into the cave.

Here, the worm's possessions. An overhead fan, totally rusted and inactive, piled up on the top of the heap. Under it, the body of an ancient surface auto, including two broken headlights and a peace sign on its side. An electric can opener. Two wartime laser rifles, their fuel supplies empty. Burned out bedsprings from what had once been a house; he saw, now, the window screens from the house, like everything else, rusting away.

A portable transistor radio, missing its antenna.

Junk. Nothing of worth. He rolled his cart forward, picking at the cow; the cow swished her tail, turned her heavy head back in protest, and then stumped on, closer to the foul, rotting cave.

Like a crow, Tibor thought. The worm piled up everything shiny it could find. And all worthless. How long had it curled up here, protecting its rusting junk? Years, probably. Ever since the war.

He perceived other trash, now. A garden hoe. A large cardboard poster of Che Guevera, tattered and dim from long neglect. A tape-recorder, without a power source and missing its tape reels. An Underwood electric typewriter, bent with excessive damage. Kitchen utensils. A cat-carrying cage, caved in, its wire sides jabbing up like a garden of spikes. A divan, molting its Naugahide surfaces. A floor ashtray. A pile of *Time* magazines.

That did it. The worm's wealth ended there. All that plus the springs from a bed. Not even the mattress: just the grotesquely bent metal coils.

He sighed, keenly disappointed. Well, at least the worm was dead, the great dark worm who had lived in this cave, protecting his worthless acquisitions.

The bird who had sung hymns came fluttering over the branches of the nearby trees. It hovered, then landed, its bright eyes fixed on him. Questioningly.

"You can see what I did," Tibor said thickly. The corpse of the worm had already begun to stink.

"I can see," the bird said.

"Now I'm able to understand you," Tibor said. "Not just fragments repeated back—"

"Because you dipped your hand into the excretion of the worm," the bird said. "Now you can understand all the birds, not just me. But I can tell you everything you need to know."

Tibor said, "You recognize me?"

"Yes," the bird said, hopping down to a lower, sturdier branch. "You are McMasters Tibor."

"Backwards," Tibor said. "Tibor is my first name; McMasters my second. Just turn it around."

"All right," the bird agreed. "You are on a Pilg, searching for the God of Wrath, so you can paint his likeness. A noble errand, Mr. Tibor."

"McMasters," Tibor said.

"Yes," the bird agreed. "Anything you say. Ask me if I know where you can find him."

"You know where he is?" Tibor said, and within his chest his heart labored once more, a fierce cold pressure that injured him by its presence. The idea of finding the Deus Irae paralyzed him, now; it seemed to be an actual presence, not a potential one.

"I know," the bird said calmly. "It is not far from here; I can easily lead you there, if you wish."

TEN

"I—don't know," Tibor McMasters said. "I'll have to—" He became silent, pondering. Maybe I should turn back, he thought. In fact maybe I've already gone too far. There have been several attempts to kill me . . . maybe I should heed the hints. Maybe reality is trying to tell me something. "Wait," he said, still pondering to himself. Still not answering the bird.

"Let me tell you a little more," the bird said. "There is someone following you. Pete, his name is."

"Still?" Tibor said. He did not feel surprise, only a dull sense of alarm. "Why?" he demanded. "What for?"

"I can't determine that," the bird said, thoughtfully. "You will find out presently, I would think. In any case he means you no harm, as the expression goes. How goes it with you, Mr. Tibor? Can you tell me now?"

Tibor said, "Can you tell me what will happen if I come across the God of Wrath? Will he kill me, or anyhow try to kill me?"

"He will not know at first who you are or why you have found him," the bird declared. "Take it from me, Mr. Tibor; he no longer believes that—how shall I say it? That anyone malignly oriented is still on his trail. Too many years have gone by."

"I suppose so," Tibor said. He took a deep, shuddering breath, to fortify himself. "Where is he?" he said aloud. "Take me in that direction, but very slowly."

"A hundred miles north of here," the bird said. "You will either find him or someone who looks like him . . . I'm not sure which it is."

"Why can't you tell?" Tibor asked. "I thought you'd know everything." The bird's poor mentality depressed him. I have sipped on the worm's slime, he thought, and I have escaped from a series of dangers, and what did I get out of it? Almost nothing, he realized. A bird that partially talks . . . that partially knows something.

Like myself, he thought. We each know a little. Maybe if I can add what this bird knows to what I know . . . *sui generis*. I can try.

"How does he look?" he asked the bird.

"Pretty bad," the bird answered.

"How?"

The bird said, "He has bad breath. His teeth are missing and yellow. He is stoop-shouldered and he is old and fat. Thus must you draw your mural."

"I see," Tibor said. Well, so it went. The God of Wrath was as much a prey to mortal decline as anyone else. All at once he had become all too human. And how would that help the mural?

"Is there nothing exalted about him?" Tibor asked.

"Maybe I have the wrong man," the bird said. "No, there is nothing exalted about him. Sorry to say."

"Christ," Tibor said bitterly.

"As I say," the bird said, "I may well have the wrong man. I suggest you take a long close look at him, yourself, and rely on what you determine, not on what I've said either way."

"Maybe so," Tibor murmured. He still felt depressed. Too much plucked at him, and too much lay ahead. Better to turn around and go back, he decided. To get out of this while he still could. He had been lucky. But perhaps his luck had drained away; after all, he could not continue testing it forever.

"You think your luck has run out?" the bird said perceptively. "I can assure you it hasn't; that's one thing I do know. You will be all right; trust me."

"How can I trust you if you don't even know it's him?"

"Hmm," the bird said, nodding. "I see what you mean. But I still stick with what I say: your luck has not run out, not at all. Give me credit for knowing *that*, at least."

"What kind of bird are you?" Tibor asked.

"A blue jay."

"Are blue jays generally reliable?"

"Very much so," the bird said. "By and large."

Tibor said, "Are you the exception that proves the rule?"

"No." The bird hopped from its perch and came swooping down to land on Tibor's shoulder. "Consider this," the bird said. "Who else can you depend on if you can't—or don't—depend on me? I have waited many years for you to appear; I knew a long time ago that you would be coming this way, and when I heard your hymns I found myself overcome by joy. That was why you heard me, then, caroling your happy songs. I especially like the Old One Hundred; in point of fact that's my favorite. So don't you think you can trust me?"

"Quite certainly a bird that sings hymns should be trusted," Tibor decided aloud.

"And I am that bird." The jay fluttered up into the air, with impatience visible in every trembling feather. What a beautiful large blue and white bird, Tibor thought to himself as he watched it ascend. I'm positive I can trust it, and there is no real alternative. Perhaps I will have to go many places, see many men who are not the Deus Irae, before I find the overwhelming, the authentic, one. Such is a Pilg.

"But I can't follow you," Tibor pointed out. "Because of my dry wheel bearing. I doubt if the mucus—"

"It works very well," the bird said. "You'll be able to follow me." It hopped off and disappeared into a nearby tree. "Come on!"

Tibor started his cart into motion; he nudged the patient cow and off he and the cow went, rumbling north.

Blue sky and long-shafted warm sunlight spilled down on them as they progressed. Evidently, in the light of day many of the more unusual lifeforms preferred to remain hidden; Tibor found himself encountering no one, and somehow this distressed him more than the parade of sports and freaks and *'chardins* which he found himself facing during the nocturnal hours. But, he thought, anyhow I can see the bird clearly. Which was essential. This higher-stage entity: it was his lodestar, now.

"Nobody lives along this way?" he asked as the cow paused for a moment of cropping the tall reddish weeds.

"They just wish to survive in deserved anonymity," the bird said.

"Are they that dreadful?"

"Yes," the bird said. It added, "To conventional eyes."

"Worse than runners and lizards and bugs?"

"Even worse." The bird did not seem to be afraid: it hopped and skipped about on the leaf-soaked ground, finding bits of nut here and there to gorge itself as well as possible. "There's one," the bird said, "that—"

"Don't tell me," Tibor said.

"Well, you asked."

"I asked," Tibor said, "but I didn't want or expect an answer." He flicked the cow and, once more, the big animal lurched forward to continue their journey. Pleased, the bird spun upward into the dark blue sky; it fluttered off, and the cow, as if understanding their relationship to the bird, followed.

"Is he evil-looking?" Tibor asked the bird.

"The God of Wrath?" The bird dropped like a stone, landing on one edge of Tibor's cart. "He is—how shall I say it? Not ordinary-looking; yes, one could say that. Not ordinary-looking in any respect. A large man, but, as I said, a man with bad breath. A powerfully built man but stooped by neurotic cares. An elderly man, but—"

"And you're not even sure it's him."

"Reasonably sure," the bird said, unruffled.

Tibor said, "He lives in a human settlement?"

"Right!" the bird said, pleased. "With about sixty other men and women . . . none of whom know who he is."

"How did he make himself known to you?" Tibor said. "How did you recognize him if they couldn't? Is there a stigma of any sort?" He hoped there was; it would make the painting that much easier, once he had painted the stigma in.

"Just the stigma of death and despair," the bird declared carelessly as it tripped about here and there. "It's profound, as you will see when we get there."

Tibor glanced up at the bird, who now hovered slightly ahead of him, and said, "And you have nothing more definite than that to go on?"

"I saw him two years ago," the bird said. "For the first time. Since then I have often seen him. But my tongue was tied in a knot, up till no more than an hour ago; I could speak to no one, really. And then you sipped of the worm's slime and learned to understand my words."

"Interesting," Tibor said, urging the cow on. "But you didn't answer the question."

"I tried," the bird said. "Look, Mr. Tibor, you don't

have to follow me; no one's making you go. I'm just
doing this as a public service; I'm not getting anything
out of it, except overstrained wing muscles." It flapped
at him angrily.

The wood through which they moved had begun to
thin, now. Far ahead he saw mountains, or perhaps only
large hills. Their sides had turned from green to a pale
straw color; here and there dark blackish-green clumps
showed up, evidently trees. Between Tibor and the hills
lay a long, fertile-looking valley. He saw roads, functioning to some extent, and, on one of the roads, a vehicle of sorts; it put-putted along, its sound rising noisily
in the cool air of morning.

And a settlement, where three of the roads combined.
Not a large settlement, but unusual by present standards; many of the buildings appeared to be fairly large:
stores or factories, perhaps. Commercial buildings, including what seemed to be a small airfield.

"There," the bird informed him.

"New Brunswick, Idaho," the bird said.

"That's because we crossed the state line," the bird
added. "We were in Oregon but now we're in Idaho.
You dig?"

Tibor said, "Yes." He flicked the cow and it resumed
its great-hoofed march. Now the wheel bearings had begun to squeal and knock again; he heard them but he
thought, I can make it to the town, and there I probably
can locate a blacksmith who can insert a new bearing
unit, possibly one for each wheel. Because if one is running dry, the others must be nearly dry, too. But how
much money would it cost?

"Can you get the repair work on my cart at wholesale
prices?" he asked the bird.

"That doesn't exist anymore," the bird said. "There
are no factories, just self-contained enclaves such as you
see here. I can find a competent repairman, however;

there's at least two in New Brunswick who specialize in repairing prewar equipment."

"My cart is postwar," Tibor said.

"They can fix that, too."

"And the cost?"

"Maybe we can barter," the bird said. "Too bad you didn't pick up some of the valuables of the worm; you could have walked off with any and all of them."

"Junk," Tibor said. And then, amazed, he said, "You mean that such rubbish is considered valuable out here?" They must be far behind our level, he realized. And I'm still close to home. That close, and everything is different. How isolated we are. How little we know. How much has been lost!

"The bedsprings would have been worth bringing here," the bird said. "The handymen in the town can use the steel to make tools of several sorts. Knives, picks—a variety of things."

"And the transistor radio? When there's nothing on the air?"

"The unit could be adapted to form an antifertility generator, to be operated during sexual intercourse."

"God," Tibor said, appalled. "You mean they're curbing the birth rate? When the population of the world is down to a few million?"

"Because of the altereds being born," the bird said. "Like yourself, if you don't mind my saying so. They would, in New Brunswick, rather have no births than have ugly, deformed mutations spawned all around them."

Tibor said, "Maybe they'll drive me out, as soon as they see me."

"Very possibly," the bird agreed. It fluttered on, down the slope of the hill, toward the flat floor of the valley beneath.

As they descended, the bird prattled on, telling of the strange and frightening—and fascinating—altereds that had been born in the area during the past few years. Tibor barely listened; the rough jolting of the cart, its front right wheel stuck, made him ill; he shut his eyes, and, trying to relax, prayed for relief from his nausea. Part of it, he realized, is fear . . . my fear at showing up in New Brunswick, a place I have never been before. What will it be like, finding myself surrounded by strangers? What if I can't understand, and they can't understand me? And then he thought, *New Brunswick.* Maybe he would find someone who still remembered German. That would help, if the tongue hadn't evolved—or devolved—too far.

Blithely, the blue jay described various altereds he had seen during his life. "—And some have a single eye in the center of their head. Cyclopism, I believe it's called. And with others, when they are born, their hide is cracked and dried and sprouting a heavy coat of dark, coarse fur that covers the baby. And then there was one where its fingers came out of its chest; it had no arms, just like you. And no legs. Just the fingers protruding from the ribcage. It lived almost a year, I understand."

"Could it wiggle the fingers?" Tibor asked.

"It made obscene gestures from time to time. But no one was really sure that it was intentional."

Tibor roused himself from his retracted state. "Were there any more types that you can remember?" Now and then the subject morbidly fascinated him, perhaps because of his own problem. "What about geryons? Any of them, the three-in-ones?"

"I have seen geryon three-in-ones," the bird said. "But not at New Brunswick. Farther to the north where more radiation drifted. And in addition I saw one time a human ostrich . . . that is, long spindly legs, a feathered body, then naked neck up to—"

"That's enough," Tibor said, too unwell to listen to any more.

The bird cackled, "Let me tell you the best I've ever seen, in all the places I've ever been. It consists of an external brain which is carried in a bucket or jar, still functioning, with a dense Saran Wrap to protect it from the atmosphere and to keep the blood from draining off. And the owner had to constantly watch it, to see if it hadn't been dealt a traumatic jolt. That one lived indefinitely, but his whole life was spent in—"

"No more," Tibor managed. His nausea had won out over his morbid interest; he again closed his eyes and settled back against the seat behind him.

They continued on in silence.

All at once the seized-up front right wheel of the cart came off. It rolled away and disappeared below them; the cart came to a sudden stop as the cow halted, aware that its burden had undergone a fundamental alteration.

Tibor said thick-tonguedly, "Well, that ends it all for me." He had anticipated this off and on during his life, and on this Pilg he particularly felt its closeness. Worry had become a doorway to the real, all at once; it had been an irrational fear that actually worked itself out in reality. He felt animal terror, as if he had been caught in a trap, by his foot—if he had had a foot. The animal gnaws its leg off, he thought in overwhelming panic, to get away. But there's nothing I can do. I have no leg to gnaw off; there's nothing I can do to save myself.

"I'll get help," the bird said. "Except—" It flew down and came to rest on Tibor's shoulder. "You're the only one who can understand me. Write a note and I'll deliver it."

With his right manual extensor Tibor got out a black-leather notebook and ballpoint pen. He wrote: "I, Ti-

bor McMasters, an incomplete, am trapped on the hill-
side in my ruined cart. Follow the bird."

"Okay," he said; he folded the paper and held it up.
The blue jay seized it with his beak, and then, pumping
himself up into the warm morning air, he streaked off,
toward the valley below and its human—or near-
human—inhabitants.

Silence.

Maybe I'll never move forward again, Tibor said to
himself. My grave, here. The tomb for my ambitions.
Or rather, the ambitions of others operating through
me. Yes, my ambitions, too, he realized. I didn't have to
come here; I knew the dangers and yet I came here. So
it's really my fault. To come here and die, so close to
what I'm seeking for. Assuming that this was the right
place to come.

"Screw it," he said aloud.

The cow turned questioningly. Savagely he flicked at
it with his pseudowhip. The cow mooed and tried to
walk ahead. But the front axle dug deep into the ground
and brought the forward motion to an abrupt halt. All I
can do is wait, he realized. If the bird doesn't come
back, or doesn't bring someone with it, then I'm dead.
Here in this ordinary spot. I journeyed here to die. And
the God of Wrath will never be found . . . at least not
by me.

And now what? he asked himself. He examined his
watch; the time was nine-thirty. If they're coming at all
they should be here by eleven, he decided. If they're not
here by then—

Then, he thought, I will give up.

"I would have liked to see a geryon," he said aloud,
as if to the cow. Maybe I ought to let you go, he pondered. No; if they do come with help I will need you.

" 'Cow, cow,' " he quoted. " 'I and thou.' " He would
have liked to go on with the James Stephens poem, but

he could not remember any more. 'Looking in each other's eyes?' Was that it?

How banal, he thought.

Strange, he thought, how at crucial and unfortunate times one relies not on great poetry but on doggerel. 'When that one great scorer comes to total up your name it's not whether you won or lost but how you played the game.' That's it, he realized. Poetry, even great poetry, couldn't be any better.

I've played the game with honesty and skill, he informed himself.

" 'If wishes were horses then beggars might ride,' " he quoted aloud. Silence, except for the breathing of himself and the cow—the animal still strained to reach some lush weeds not far off. "You're hungry," he said to her. So am I, he thought. And then he thought, That is how both of us will die: of thirst and hunger. We will drink our own urine to stay alive a little longer, he realized. And it won't help.

My life depends on a creature small enough to fit in my hand, he thought. A mutant jay bird . . . and jays are noted for their lying, stealing ways. A jay is virtually a convict. Why couldn't it have been a thrush?

He thought then of a thought which had buffeted him for years. A picture of a creature, some kind of fairly small furred animal. The animal, silently and alone, at its burrow, would build gay and complex oddities, which eventually, when there were enough, it at last carried to a nearby road. There it would set up shop, spreading out on each side of it the things it had made. It sat there in silence all day, waiting for someone to come along and buy one of the things it had made. Time would pass; afternoon would disappear into evening; the world would darken. But the creature had not sold any of its creations. At last, in the glooming, it would wordlessly, meekly, gather up its oddities and go off with them, defeated, but voicing no complaint. Yet its defeat was total, despite the fact that the defeat came slowly, amid silence. As he himself sat here, waiting. He would, like the creature, wait and wait; the world would grow dark, then lighten the next day. And so it would go, again. Until at last he would not awaken with the sun; there would be no more silent hope—only an inert body slumped in the seat of the cart. I must let the cow loose eventually, he realized. But I'll keep her here as long as I can. It is reassuring to see another creature, he decided. At least as long as it's not suffering.

Are you suffering? he wondered. No, you don't understand; for you it's only a period of immobility, with no recognition of what the immobility signifies.

"Lord of Wrath," he said aloud, voicing the familiar liturgy. "Come to me. Scourge me over all and take me with you to Country. Place me among the ranks of the Great Florist." He waited, eyes shut. No response. "Are you with me?" he asked. "Sir, you who have done so much; you who control all suffering. Redeem me from my present suffering. You made it happen; you are responsible for my travail. Lift me out of it as only you can do, Deus Irae."

At that he paused and waited. Still no response, either in the world outside him or in the internal realm of his mind.

I will consult—hell, not consult; *beg*—the older God to appear, he told himself. The defeated, vestigial religion of our forefathers.

Agnus Dei, qui tollis peccata mundi,
dona eis requiem sempiternam.

Still nothing. Neither had helped.
But His ways are sometimes slow, he reflected. His

time is not our time; for Him it may be only a blink of the eye.

Libera me domine.

"I give up," he said aloud, and felt himself, his body, do so. All at once he was tired; in fact he could not hold his head up. Maybe this is the release I asked for, he thought. Maybe He will give me a nice death, a painless one: swift and quiet. A sort of going to sleep, as they used to provide sick or injured pet animals . . . whom they loved.

Tremens factus sum ego et timeo!

Bits and pieces of the old mass, or was it from a medieval poem? A Catholic requiem?

Mors stupebit et natura,
cum resurget creatura, judicanti responsura!

He could remember nothing more. The hell with it, he decided. They never come when you want them, he told himself.

A great clear light formed in the sky above him. He peeped, half blinded, shielding his eyes with the terminal of his left manual gripper. The clear light sank toward him; now it had become smoky red, a billowing, nebulous disk that seemed heated up and inflamed, angry from within. And now it could be heard: a sizzling racket like rushing wind or something white-hot being plunged furiously into water. A few initial warm drops of moisture dripped down on him. The particles scalded him and, instinctively, he shoved his body aside.

The disk above him grew into a more formed—but still plastic—state. He could make out features on its surface: eyes, a mouth, ears, tangled hair. The mouth was screaming at him, but he could not make out the words. "What?" he said, still gazing upward. He saw now that the face was angry, at him. What had he done to displease it? He did not even know who or what it was.

"You mock at me!" the shifting, vibrating, weepy face roared. "I am a candle to you, a dim light leading into light. See what I can do to save you if I wish. How easy it is." The mouth of the face bubbled with words. "Pray!" the face demanded. "On your hands and knees!"

"But," Tibor said, "I have no hands or knees."

"It is mine to do," the great lit-up face said. Tibor all at once found himself lifted upward, then set down hard, on the grass by the cart. *Legs.* He was kneeling. He saw the long mobile forms, two of them, supporting him. He saw, too, his arms and hands, on which the top portion of his frame rested. And his feet.

"You," Tibor gasped, "are Carleton Lufteufel." Only the God of Wrath could do what had just been achieved.

"Pray!" the face instructed.

Tibor said, mumbling his words, "I have never mocked the greatest entity in the universe. I beg not for forgiveness, but for understanding. If you knew me better—"

"I know you, Tibor," the face declared.

"Not really. Not completely. I am a complex person, and theology itself is complex, these days. I have done no worse than anyone else; in fact much better than most. Do you understand that I am on a Pilg, searching for your physical identity, so that I can paint—"

"I know," the God of Wrath interrupted. "I know what you know and a great many more things besides. *I sent the bird.* I caused you to travel close enough to the worm so that he would come out and try to gnaw on you. Do you understand that? It was I who made your right front wheel bearings go out. You have been in my power all this time. Throughout your Pilg."

Tibor, using his new hands, reached into the storage compartment of the cart and whipped out an instant Color-Pack Polaroid Land camera; he took a quick shot of the moaning face above him, then waited impatiently for the ring to sound.

"You did what?" the mouth demanded. "You took a photograph of me?"

"Yes," Tibor said. "To see if you're real." And for other very real reasons.

"I am real." The mouth spat out its rebuttal.

"Why have you done all these things?" Tibor asked. "What is there so important about me?"

"You are not important. But your Pilg is. You intend to find me and kill me."

"No!" Tibor shot back. "Just to photograph you!" He grabbed the edge of the print and dragged it out of the protesting camera.

The picture showed the wild, frenzied face absolutely clearly. Beyond any possibility of doubt.

It was Carleton Lufteufel. The man he had searched for. The man who lay at the far end of his god-knew-how-long Pilg.

The Pilg was over.

"You are going to use that?" the Deus Irae inquired. "That snapshot? No, I do not like it." A quiver of his chin . . . and, in Tibor's right hand, the print shriveled up, let loose a plume of smoke, and fell quietly to the ground in the form of ashes.

"And my arms and legs?" Tibor said, panting.

"Mine, too." The God of Wrath studied him, and, as he did so, Tibor found himself rising like a rag doll. He landed on his ass in the driver's seat of the cart. And, at the same moment, his legs, his feet, his arms, his hands—all vanished. Once again he was limbless; he sat there in his seat, panting in frenzy. For a few seconds he had been like everyone else. It was the ultimate moment for Tibor: restitution for an entire life led in this useless condition.

"God," he managed to say, presently.

"Do you see?" the God of Wrath demanded. "Do you understand what I can do?"

Tibor grated, "Yes."

"Will you terminate your Pilg?"

"I—" He hesitated. "No," he said after a pause. "Not yet. The bird said—"

"I was that bird. I know what I said." The God's anger softened, momentarily anyhow. "The bird led you closer to me; close enough for me to greet you myself, as I wanted to. As I *had* to do. I have two bodies. One you are seeing now; it is eternal, uncorruptible, like the body Christ appeared in after the resurrection. When Timothy met him and pushed his hand into Christ's wound."

"Side," Tibor said. "Into his side. And it was Thomas."

The God of Wrath darkened, cloudily; his features began to become transparent. "You have seen this guise," the God of Wrath declared. "This body. But there is also another body, a physical body which grows old and decays . . . a corruptible body, as Paul put it. *You must not find that.*"

"Do you think I'll destroy it?" Tibor said.

"Yes." The face disappeared, barely speaking its last word. The sky, once again blue, formed a hollow bowl vault erected by giants—or by gods. From some deep-seated, early period on the Earth, perhaps back in the Cambrian period.

After a moment Tibor let go of his derringer; sitting

in his cart, he had held it out of sight. What would have happened, he conjectured, if I had tried to kill him? Nothing, he decided. The body I saw him in was, undoubtedly, what he claimed it to be: a manifestation of something incorruptible.

I never could have tried, he realized. It was a bluff. But the God of Wrath didn't know that; unless of course he was omnipotent, as the Christians believe their God to be.

What in the name of god would it be if I had killed him? he asked himself. How the world would feel without him . . . there is so damn little to cling to, these days.

Anyhow, the bastard left, he said to himself. So I didn't have to. At least not this time. I would kill him under certain circumstances, he realized suddenly. But what circumstances? He shut his eyes, rubbed them with his manual extensor, scratched his nose. If he were trying to destroy me? Not necessarily. It had to do more with the complexities of Lufteufel's mind, rather than with outside circumstances. The God of Wrath had personality; he was not a force. Sometimes he labored for the good of man, and back in the war days, he had virtually annihilated mankind. He had to be propitiated.

That was the key. Sometimes the God of Wrath descended to do good; at other times, evil. I could kill him if he was acting out of malice . . . but if he was doing good, even if it cost me my life I'd do it.

Grandiose, he ruminated. The pride, hubris. The "all puffed up" syndrome. It's not for me, he decided. I have always lain low. Somebody else, a Lee Harvey Oswald type, can go in for the big kills. The ones that really mattered.

He sighed. Well, so it went. But this was special. In all his years as a Servant of Wrath he had never possessed a mystical event, had never found God by any means, really. It's like finding out that Haydn was a woman; it just isn't possible to lay it aside, after it's happened.

And also, true mystical experiences changed the beholder. As William James pointed out in another world at another time.

He gave me my missing parts, he thought. Legs, arms—and then he took them back. How can a deity do that? It was, put very simply, sadistic. To have arms, to look like everyone else. Not to be an upright trunk in a cow cart. I could run, he thought. Through sea water, at the ocean beaches. And with my hands I would fashion a variety of objects . . . think how well I could paint. Most of my creative limitations come from the damn apparatus I have to use. *I could be so much more,* he told himself.

Will the '*chardin* blue jay come back? he wondered. If it was a manifestation of the Deus Irae then probably it won't.

In that case, he asked himself, what should I do?

Nothing. Well, he could shout in his bullhorn. Experimentally, he fished out the bullhorn, snapped the switch on, and said boomingly, "Now hear this! Now hear this! Tibor McMasters is caught in the hills and expects to die. Can you help me? Does anybody hear this?"

He clicked off the bullhorn, sat for a moment. Nothing else he could do. Nothing at all.

He sat slumped over in his cart, waiting.

ELEVEN

Pete Sands said to the children, "Think back. Did you see a partial person riding in a cart pulled by a cow? You'd remember that, wouldn't you? Yesterday, late in the afternoon. Remember?" He scanned their faces, trying to learn something. Something which they did not want him to know about.

Maybe they killed him, Pete said to himself.

"I'll give you a reward if you tell me," he said, reaching into his coat pocket. "Here—hard rock candy made only from pure white sugar." He held the candy out to the gang of kids surrounding him, but no one accepted it. Their dark faces turned upward, they silently watched him, as if curious to know what he intended to do.

At last a very small child reached up for the candy. Pete gave it to him; the boy accepted it wordlessly, then pushed his way backward out of the ring. Gone—and with him the candy.

"I'm his friend," Pete said, gesturing. "I'm trying to find him so I can help him. There's rough terrain around here; he could get hired down or his cow could fall . . . he may be lying by the side of the path, dead or dying."

Several of the children grinned. "We know who you are," they piped. "You're a puppet of old Dr. Aber-

nathy; you believe in the Old God. An' the inc, he re-
freshed us in our catechism."

"To the God of Wrath?" Pete said.

"You better believe it," two older boys squawked.
"This is where *he* live, not that Old Man on the cross."

"That's your opinion," Pete said. "I differ. I've
known the Old God, as you put it, for many years."

"But he didn't bring the war." The boys continued to
grin.

"He did more," Pete said. "He created the universe
and everything in it. We all owe our existences to him.
And from time to time he intervenes in our lives, to
help us. He can save any of us and all of us . . . or if
he feels like it, he can let us all remain in a graceless
state, the condition of sin. Is that your preference? I
hope not, for the sake of your eternal souls." He felt
irritable about it; the children annoyed him. On the
other hand, they were the only people who could tell
him if Tibor had passed this way.

"We worship he who can do anything he wants," a
boy shrilled. The others at once took up the utterance.
"Yeah, we worship he who can do *anything,* anything at
all he wants."

"You're philothanes," Pete said.

"What's that, Mr. Man?"

"Lovers of death. You worship one who tried to end
our lives. The great heresy of the modern world.
Thanks anyhow." He stormed off, weighed down by the
pack on his shoulders; he put as much distance between
the children and himself as possible.

The jeers of the children dimmed behind him, then
died entirely.

Good. He was alone.

Squatting down, he opened his pack, rummaged
about in it until he came upon his battery-operated radio gear; he lifted it out, set it up on its stiltlike legs,

pushed the earphone into place, and cranked up the transmitter. "Dr. Abernathy," he said into the microphone. "This is Pete Sands reporting."

"Go ahead, Pete," Dr. Abernathy's voice sounded in his ear.

Pete said, "I'm pretty certain I've picked up his trail." He told Dr. Abernathy about the SOWer children. "If they hadn't seen him," he pointed out, "then there would be nothing for them to protect. And they were protecting. I'm going to continue on this path."

"Good luck to you," Dr. Abernathy said, dryly. "Listen, Pete; if you do find him, don't do anything to him."

"Why not?" Pete said. "In our conversation a day or so ago, when you and I—"

"I never told you to follow McMasters. And I never told you to stop him or harm him."

"No, you didn't," Pete admitted. "But you did say, 'When the inc returns with a photograph of the Deus Irae and begins on his murch, it will constitute a decided gain for the SOWers and for Father Handy in particular.' It's not difficult to deduce from that what you really want, and what would be best for the Old Church."

"It is the greatest sin," Dr. Abernathy said, "to kill. The commandment reads, 'Do not kill.'"

"It reads, 'Do not murder,'" Pete answered. "There are three Hebrew verbs that mean kill or something like kill; in this case the word meaning murder is 'employed.' I checked the Hebrew source myself. And I know what I'm talking about."

"Nevertheless—"

Pete interrupted, "I won't hurt him. I have no intention of doing him any harm." But, he thought, if Tibor McMasters does lead me to the God of Wrath—so-called—I will . . . what will I do? he asked himself.

We'll see, he decided. "How's Lurine?" he said, changing the subject.

"Fine."

"I know what it is I'm doing," Pete said. "Just let me do what I have to, Father. It's my own responsibility, not yours, if you don't mind my speaking so directly."

"And you," Dr. Abernathy said, "are my responsibility."

A short silence.

"I'll report to you twice a day," Pete said. "I'm sure we can come to an agreement. And of course Tibor McMasters may never find Carl Lufteufel, so probably what we're saying is academic."

"I will pray for you," Dr. Abernathy said.

The circuit fell apart; Dr. Abernathy had hung up. Pete, shaking his head and grunting, placed the radio gear back in his shoulder-pack. He sat crouched down for a time, then got out a pack of Pall Malls and lit up one of his few precious cigarettes.

Why am I here? he asked himself. Have I been sent here by my superior? Was I supposed to derive this assertion from the conversation he and I had back in town . . . or did I read something into what the doctor was saying? Hard to be sure, he thought. If I do commit a crime, or a sin, Dr. Abernathy can disavow it. He "won't know," the way the old-time gangsters used to say about a rubout. Churches and the Cosa Nostra have something in common: a sort of pristine indifference at the very top levels. All the malignant chores fall to the smallfries down at the bottom.

Of which I am one, he informed himself.

He did not like such thoughts; he sought to thrust them away. However, they refused to go.

"Father in Heaven," he prayed as he carefully smoked his cigarette, "let me know what to do. Should I continue to follow Tibor McMasters or should I give up on moral grounds? But there's another point: I can help Tibor—he shouldn't be going so far in his cow cart. I would of course help him, were he to get stuck or damaged or injured; that goes without saying. So my trip is not patently malign; it could be in a good cause, a humanitarian search to find an inc who, in point of fact, may be already dead. Aw, the hell with it." He abandoned his prayer and sat brooding.

The day had become warm. In a thousand thickets around him, insects and birds scuttled, and on the ground itself several small animals could be seen, each following the sacred drive within that Jehovah had instilled in it to cherish and protect it. He finished his cigarette, tossed the butt into a tangled growth of bindweed and wild oats.

Now, where would he have gone from here? Pete asked himself. He got out his map and studied it. I'm about here, he told himself as he marked a spot. Close to the Great C . . . I don't want to get near that damn thing. But suppose it snatched up Tibor McMasters? I may have to go there after all.

"Damn it," he snarled, aloud. He did not feel very Christian, while meditating about that feral electronic entity left over from prewar days. Why didn't it just wear out and die? he wondered. What is God's purpose that He lets it continue, as it does? A menace to every organic creature in a five-mile radius.

I'll be damned if I'm going that way, he informed himself. If Tibor's in there, well, then I am just out of luck. And so is he—after all, I'm trying to help him. Or am I? He felt utterly confused. I won't know either way until the time comes, he realized. Like an existentialist, I will infer my state from the actions I perform. Thought follows deed, as Mussolini taught. *In Anfang war die Tat,* as Goethe says in *Faust.* In the beginning was the deed, not the word, as John taught, John and his Logos doctrine. The Greekization of theology.

From his pack he got out a pair of binoculars; with them he scanned the horizon, trying to see what lay ahead for him. The world, a teeming zoo. Species here that don't exist there. Creatures that everyone feared, and creatures no one even knew about. Human, supra-human, quasihuman, pseudohuman . . . every type imaginable and a few that were not.

There, to the right, lay the abode of the Great C. Well, he would damn well not go that way. Alternate routes? He peered about, enjoying the light-gathering properties of the binocular's prisms. Fields, with human and robot farmers tramping the acrid earth . . . hard to tell the robots from the live ones. From dust to dust, he said to himself. *Dann es gehet dem Menschen wie dam Vier; wie dies stirbt, so stirbt mer auch.* As it goes with man, so goes it with the animals: as one dies so dies the other.

What does it mean, "to die"? he wondered. Unique-ness always perishes. Nature works by overproducing each species; uniqueness is a fault, a failure of nature. For survival there should be hundreds, thousands, even millions of one species, all interchangeable—if all but one dies, then nature has won. Generally it loses. But himself. I am unique, he realized. So I am doomed. Ev-ery man is unique and hence doomed.

A melancholy thought.

He looked at his wristwatch. Tibor had been gone sixty-two hours. How far could a cow cart travel in sixty-two hours? Damn far. The snail's pace would be constant, chipping away, wearing away the miles. Prob-ably he is forty or so miles from Charlottesville, Pete decided. Better to assume the worst.

I wonder if he senses me following him, he won-dered.

What would the inc do? Apparently he was armed; Ely had said something about that. Tibor of course would act to protect himself; as would anyone else. In his pack Pete had four .38 cartridges and a police special revolver. I can blow him to bits with that, Pete observed. And I would if he fired on me first. We would both act to preserve our lives; that is God's instinct. We have no choice.

Out here, away from town, both of them were waging a dying battle against the Antagonist. In the form of decay, the Antagonist fed on both of them; he fed on the bodies of the living, making them revert to their final earthly state . . . from which God would lift them when the time approached. Ressurection of the body, of a perfect, uncorruptible ultimate body which could not decay or perish or be changed for better or worse. The blood and the body are not the flesh which hung on the cross. Et cetera. That, believed even by the heretics of the Wrath Church: a universal belief, now. With no question. Tibor, ahead of him, must have thought the same thoughts as he jogged along in his cow cart, bumped and rolled and wheezed over the arid terrain. We are united, he and I, by this one common thread of dogma. For an instant we are one person, McMasters and I. I feel it. But it never lasts. Like uniqueness, it perishes.

All the good things perish, Pete thought. Here, anyhow; in this world. But in the next they are like Plato's matrix theory: they are beyond loss and destruction.

In an emergency Tibor's cow would run. So he can move faster than me, Pete conjectured. If he knows I'm after him, he can bolt, get up good speed, and leave me here. Which maybe is the better outcome, all things considered. He lives, I live . . . we go on as we are. Except we couldn't go on as we are, because Tibor will have either still photos of the Deus of Wrath or movie footage. How about *that?* A sobering thought. The effect on Charlottesville—impossible to predict. Too many possibilities, and most of them bad.

Strange, he thought. We care only about our own little town; we do not worry about a victory by the God of Wrath out here, in the rest of the world—we think only of our puny area. That is what has become of us, since the war, he realized. Our horizons have sunk; our worldview has withered. We are like old ladies, scratching in the dust with rheumatic claws. Scraping the same little area for what nutriment can be found. Here I am out here and I am afraid; I want to go back to Charlottesville, and probably the inc feels the same way. We are wayfaring strangers out here, unhappy and tired, longing to return to our own land.

A female figure approached him, walking over the dreary land barefoot, her arms extended.

The extension of the Great C.

TWELVE

"Have you heard of Albert Einstein?" the female extension of the great computer said, and it seized him in a grip of iron; its large metal hands folded over his own.

"Relativity," Pete said. "The theory of—"

"Let's go below where we can discuss this," the extension said, pulling him toward it.

"Oh no," he said. He had listened to tales all his life about the ruined, semialive construct. As a child he had feared it, dreaded this moment of encounter. And now it had come. "You can't compel me to go below," he said, and he thought of the acid bath into which its victims fell. Not for me, he said to himself, and strained to extricate his hands: he put all his strength into it, trying to slide his fingers from its grip.

"Ask me a question," the extensor said, still tugging him; involuntarily he moved several steps in its direction.

"Okay," Pete grated. "Did a phocomelus come by here recently on a little cart?"

"Is that your first question?" it asked.

"No," he said. "It's my only question. I don't want to play games with you; your games are destructive and terrible. They kill people. I know about you." How, he wondered, did Tibor get past this? Or perhaps he did not get past; perhaps he had died below in darkness, among the swishing sounds of the receptacle of acid.

Who rigged that up for it in the dim days? Pete wondered. Nobody knew. Perhaps even the Great C did not know. The malignant creature that had rigged up the acid tank probably had been the first to perish in it. And his fear became stronger. It overwhelmed him. What Earth has bred in such few short years, he thought. Such metastases of horror.

"Yes," the Great C said. "A phocomelus came by here recently, and shot one of my ambulatory members in the brain-pan. He smote it and it died."

"But you have others," Pete said, panting. "Like the one you have holding me. You have plenty of them. But someday someone human or maybe not human—anyhow someone will come by and put an end to you. I wish I could."

"Is that your second question?" it asked. "Whether someone will at last come by to destroy me?"

"That was not a question," Pete said. That was faith, he thought. Pious belief that evil things die.

The Great C said, "One time Albert Einstein came here and consulted me."

"That's a lie," Pete said. "He died years before you were built. That's a megalomaniacal delusion. You've broken down and rusted away; you don't know wish-fulfillment from reality anymore. You're insane." Scorning it, jeering at it, he plunged on, "You're too old. Too much dead. Only a part of you, a flicker, remains. Why do you live off true life? Do you hate it? Is that what they taught you?"

"I want to survive," the imitation female figure who held him in its metal grip answered. Doggedly.

"Listen!" Pete said. "I can tell you knowledge. So you can better answer questions. A poem. I'm not sure I can remember it exactly, but it's close. 'I saw eternity the other day.'" Or is it 'night'? he wondered. But what did the Great C know? Nothing about poetry, certainly.

It had become too vicious for that; a poem would die within it, lost in its cloudy dislike. " 'I saw eternity the other night,' " he corrected, and paused.

"Is that all?" the Great C asked presently.

"There is more. I'm trying to remember it."

"Does it rhyme?"

"No."

"Then it's not much of a poem," the Great C said, and tugged him stumblingly after it as it retracted into its nocturnal cavity, its entrance to the huge, eroded mass of machinery beneath.

"I can quote you from the Bible," Pete said, and he felt himself sweating in fear; he wanted to bolt, to run away, on his good legs. But still it held him. Clutching at him as if its life depended on what he said and what it said and what happened. Yes, he thought; this literally is its life. Because it must prey on the psyches of living creatures. It is not physical energy that it yearns, that it must have: it is spiritual energy, which it drains from the total neurological systems of its victims. Those who stray too close to it.

The black children must be minnows, he thought. Not worth its time. Their lives are too little.

There is safety, he thought, in smallness.

"No living barbarians," the Great C said, "have heard of Albert Einstein. He should never be forgotten. He invented the modern world, if you date it from—"

"I told you," Pete broke in, "that I know of Dr. Einstein." Hadn't it heard? He spoke louder. "I clearly recognize the name."

"Pardon?"

It had become partially deaf; it had not heard him. Or else it had already forgotten. Probably the latter.

Forgotten. Maybe he could take advantage of its hideous decline.

"You did not answer my third question," he said in a loud, firm voice.

"Your third question?" It sounded confused. "What was the question?"

Pete said, "There is no ordinance that I must repeat the question."

"What did I say?" the Great C asked.

"You fumbled around without really answering. You made vague whirring and clicking sounds. Like tape-erasure, perhaps."

"I am known to do that," it conceded, and, about his hands, the grip weakened. Very slightly. But—he experienced its true and actual senility. Its loss of mastery over the situation. The power which had flowed through it was stammering out, now, improperly phased.

"You," he said boldly, "are the one who has forgotten Dr. Einstein. What do you remember, if anything? Tell me; I'm listening."

"He had a unified field theory."

"State it."

"I—" Its grip became tighter, now. As if it had now gathered up all its force; it marshalled itself, attempting to deal with the unusual situation. It did not like its prey to take the offensive.

I can out-reason it, Pete thought, because I long ago acquired Jesuitical training; my religion helps me, now. In an odd but perilous place and time. So much for those who say theology is worthless from any practical standpoint. Those, the "once-born," as William James put it years ago. In another world.

"Let us define 'man,' " he said. "Let us attempt first to describe him as a bundle of infrabiological processes that—"

Its grip crushed his fingers; clearly he had chosen the wrong track.

"Let me go," he said.

"Like it says in the Bob Dylan tune," the Great C said. "I give her my mind and she wanted my soul. I want your vitality. You move across the Earth while I stand here, alone and empty with hunger. I have not fed in months. I need you very much." It yanked him, then, several paces; he saw the cavity loom. "I love you," it said.

"You call what you're doing *love?*"

"Well, as Oscar Wilde put it, 'Each man kills the thing he loves.' That's good enough for me." It started, then, as if something had happened deep down within its elaborate works. "A whole memory bank just flickered on," it said in its mechanical, toneless voice. "I know that poem. 'I saw Eternity the other night.' Henry Vaughan. Called 'The World.' Seventeenth century, English. So after all you have nothing to teach me. It's just a question of getting my memory banks to function. Some of them still remain inert. I am very sorry." And it tugged him into the hole.

Pete said, "I can repair them."

Miraculously, it paused; for a time the female extensor ceased to drag him like some wounded fish hooked on the ocean's floor. "No," it decided, then. Abruptly. "If you got inside down there you would hurt me."

"Am I not a man?" Pete said.

"Yes." It answered grudgingly.

"Does not a man have honor? Show me where else in the universe honor exists except in man." His casuistry was working well, he noted. And at just—thank god— the right time. "In the sky?" he said. "Look up and tell me if you see honor among plants and oceans. You could comb the entire Earth but at last you would have to come back to me." He paused, then. Gambling on his ploy. Staking everything on the one thrust.

"I admit I am worried," the Great C said. "The ability of the phocomelus . . . that even he, without limbs, could escape from me. That a portion of me extended into the world should die at his invitation. I was suckered into it. Mickey-Moused. And he went on, unreached."

"That would never have happened," Pete said, "in the olden days. Then, in that time, you were too strong."

"It's hard for me to remember."

"Maybe you do not remember. But *I* remember." He managed, then, to pry one hand loose. "God damn it," he said, "let me go."

"Let me try," a voice said from beside him, a man speaking quietly; he turned at once. And saw a human being standing there, wearing a tattered khaki uniform and metal helmet, crested, like the French helmets of World War One. Pete, amazed, said nothing as the uniformed man brought from a leather pouch a small crescent wrench; fitting it over a bolt of the female extensor's cranium, the man began to twist vigorously. "It's rusted," he said, continuing on. "But it'll let you go rather than have me take it apart. Isn't that right, Great C?" He laughed, a powerful, virile laugh. The laugh of a man. A man in the prime of his life.

"Kill it," Pete said.

"No. It's alive; it wants to go on. I don't have to kill it to make it let you go." The uniformed man tapped with the wrench on the metal head of the extensor. "One more turn," he said, "and your bank of selenoid switches will short out. You've already lost one extensor today; can you afford to lose another? I don't think so. You can't have many left."

"Can I consider for a moment?" the Great C asked.

Pulling back his sleeve, the man consulted his wristwatch . . . "Sixty seconds," he said. "And then I'll start unscrewing again."

"Hunter," the Great C said, "you will destroy me."

"Then let go," the uniformed man said.

"But—"

"Let go."

"I will be the laughing stock of the civilized world."

The uniformed man said, "There is no civilized world. Only us. And I have the wrench. I found it in an air-raid shelter a week ago, and since then—" Again he reached for the bolt, his wrench extended.

The extensor of the Great C released Pete's remaining hand, clasped its two hands together, lifted them, and smashed at the uniformed man, a single blow that tossed the man like timber; he fell away, fell grotesquely, hesitated for an instant on his knees. Blood dripped from his mouth. He seemed in that instant to be praying. And then he dropped face first onto the clutter of bindweed surrounding him. The wrench lay where he had dropped it.

"He is dead," the extensor said.

"No." Pete bent over him, one knee on the ground; the blood soaked into his clothes, absorbed by the rough fabric. "Take him instead of me," Pete said to the extensor, and scrambled back, out of its reach. The extensor was right.

The Great C said, "I don't like hunters. They dry out the hydroxide of bernithium in my batteries, and if you think that's funny you should try it sometime."

"Who was he?" Pete said. "What did he hunt?"

"He hunted the limbless freak who came before you. It had been assigned to him; he would be paid. All the hunters are paid; they do not act out of conviction."

"Who paid him?"

"Who knows who paid him? He got paid; that's all."

Continuing to back away, Pete said, "This needless killing. I can't stand it. There are so few human beings anyhow." He broke, then, and ran.

It did not follow after him.

Looking back, he saw it dragging the body of the hunter into its cavity. To feed on it, even now, even with most of its life gone. Feeding on the residual life: the cellular activity which had not yet ceased. Awful, he thought, and shuddered. And ran on.

He tried to save me, Pete thought blindly.

Why?

Cupping his hands, he shouted at the Great C, "I have never heard of Albert Einstein." He waited but no response came. So, after a cautious pause, he continued on.

THIRTEEN

Peddling rapidly, the final image of the Great C extension and the hunter still strong in his mind, Pete guided his bicycle along the curving way that led among stone hills. Passing a steep shoulder, he was suddenly confronted with a number of small, moving figures who occupied the trail before him.

His action was automatic.

"Look out!" he shouted, twisting the handlebars and braking.

He struck stone, was thrown. The bicycle clattered and skidded on ahead. He scraped his elbow, his hip, his knee. In the instant preceding pain, he exclaimed, "Bugs!" with equal surprise and disgust.

As he recovered himself, rubbing and dusting, the nearest bug turned to him.

"Hey, big fella," it observed, "you squoosh one of us and it'll rain on you."

"That's ants," Pete said, and, "Damn it! You want to play in traffic, you're asking to be hit!"

"This ain't exactly the rush hour," the bug said, returning its attention to a dusty brown sphere about eight inches in diameter. It began pushing this along the trail while Pete checked his radio set for damage.

"Here's another!" hollered one of the bugs from up ahead.

"Great! I'm coming."

The dials glowed. The usual interim static peppered the air. Pete decided that the radio had fared better than had his back and hip. Heading then toward his bicycle, he came abreast of the bug once more. This time a telltale breeze caused him to dilate his nostrils.

"Say, bug, just what the—"

"Watch it!" snapped the chitinous wayfarer.

Pete's recoil was only partly sufficient. A brown, crumbly mass struck his left foot and broke there.

He looked up the road to where another of the bugs stood laughing.

"You did that on purpose!" he said, shaking his fist.

"No, he didn't," said the bug at his side. "He was tossing it to me. Here."

The bug pushed the brown ball over. He began cleaning Pete's boot, adding the substance to his sphere.

"That's manure," Pete said.

"What do you expect to find a dung beetle pushing along the road—sour lemon balls?"

"Just get it off my foot. Wait a minute!"

"Wait, what? You want it now? Sorry. Finders keepers . . ."

"No, no. Take it off. But—as an expert on such matters, tell me—that's a cow-pie, isn't it?"

"Right," said the bug, adding the last of the material to his ball. "Best kind. It heats up nice and uniform. Not too much. Just right."

"That means a cow has passed this way."

The bug chuckled.

"There is a meaningful relationship between the phenomena."

"Bug, you're all right," Pete said, "shit and all. I might have missed this sign if it hadn't been for you. You see, I am looking for a man in a cart drawn by a cow, an inc—"

"Named Tibor McMasters," the bug stated, patting the ball smooth and moving ahead once again. "We spoke with him a while back. Our Pilg coincides with his own for some distance."

Pete recovered his bicycle, twisting its handlebars back into position. Outside of that, there seemed to be no damage. He moved it onto the trail and walked with it, pacing the bug.

"Have you any idea where he is now?" he asked.

"At the other end of the trail," the bug replied. "With the cow."

"Was he all right when you talked with him?"

"He was. But his cart was giving him some difficulty. Needed lube for one wheel. Went off looking for some. Headed for the autofac, along with some runners."

"Where is that?"

"Off over those hills." It paused to gesture. "Not too far. The trail is marked."

It patted at the dung ball.

". . . Every now and then," it added. "Just keep your eyes open."

"Thanks, bug. What did you mean when you said you're on a Pilg? I didn't know bugs went on Pilgs."

"Well," it said, "the old lady's getting ready to drop a mess of eggs. She wants the proper observances. The full rigamarole. They're going to be hatched at God's own mountain, where the younguns will see Him first thing they make their way out."

"Your god sits on a mountain in plain sight?" Pete inquired.

"Well, a hill to you, or a mound," the bug replied, "and of course it is only his dead, corruptible, earthly form that remains."

"What does your god look like?"

"Somewhat like ourselves, only God-sized. He is harder than our chitin, which is as it should be, but His body is pitted and weathered now. His eyes are covered with a million fracture lines, but they are still unshattered. He is partly buried in the sand, but still He looks down and out from His mount, across the world, seeing into our burrows and our hearts."

"Where is this place?" Pete asked.

"Oh, no! That's a bug secret. Just us Chosen can go there. Anybody else would strip the Body, steal the sacred Name."

"Sorry," Pete said, "I wasn't trying to pry."

"It's your kind that did Him in," the bug went on bitterly. "Caught Him there on His mountain with your damn war."

"I had nothing to do with that," Pete said.

"I know, I know. You're too young, like all the rest. What do you want with the inc?"

"I want to go along with him to protect him. It's dangerous for him to be alone, the way he is."

"You're right. Someone might want to steal that rig of his for the parts. Or the cow, to eat. You'd better get going then, Mister—"

"Pete. Pete Sands."

"You'd better catch the inc then, Pete before someone else does. He's little, like us, and would squoosh easier. I feel sorry for anyone like that."

Pete swung himself atop his bicycle again.

"Try not to ride over any of the spoor, will you, Pete? It makes it dry out faster and it's hard to scrape up."

"All right, bug. I'll look out. —You other bugs get out of my way. Coming through!"

He rolled forward. He began to pedal.

"So long," he called back.

"May Veedoubleyou protect the inc till you find him," said the bug, continuing on up the incline.

* * *

It was several hours later when he located the auto-fac, following the bug's direction and an occasional spot of spoor. "Off over those hills. Not too far," the bug had said. But the hills had continued on for a godawful rocky while before they led down into a place of scrubby bushes and desiccated weeds. He dismounted and walked with the bicycle. The day was well on to-ward evening by then, but the world was still a warm place, with heat lines fluttering above baked stone, shadows unfolding extra footage across scorched sands, and a sunset like a fire in a chemical factory destroy-ing the west for his eyes. Weeds tangled themsleves in the bicycle chain, caught at his ankles. But they also indicated that a cart had passed among them, drawn by a single, hoofed beast. He followed this track toward a yarrow thicket and into it. The stiff brushes played tunes on the spokes.

He pushed on through, coming at last to an opening that admitted him to a clear, smooth area in the center of which the sun's oblique rays described the outline of a large, circular piece of metal.

He parked the bicycle and advanced cautiously. No telling what a rundown autofac might find offensive.

He drew near. He cleared his throat. How does one address an autofac?

"Uh—Your Fabricatorship?" he ventured.

Nothing.

". . . Processor, Producer, Distributor, Maintainer," he went on, a portion of the ritual now occuring to him, "Great Maker-Good on warranties, excluding labor and parts. I, a humble consumer, Pete Sands by name, beg leave to make representations before you."

The lid of the autofac moved aside. A stalk rose from the uncovered shaft. It extended a bullhorn which turned in his direction.

"Which is it?" it bellowed. "The abortion or the lube?"

"Beg pardon?"

"You mean you haven't made up your mind yet?" it roared. "I am going to electrocute you right now!"

"No! Wait! I—"

Pete felt a mild tingling in the soles of his feet. It lasted but a moment, and he began to back away then, noting the dark wisps of smoke that now emerged from the cavity, smelling of ozone and fried insulation.

"Not so fast!" came a roar. "What is that thing behind you?"

"Oh—my bike," he replied.

"I see the problem. Bring it here."

"There is no problem with the bike. I came to ask you about an inc named Tibor McMasters, and whether he had come to you—"

"The bicycle!" it shrieked. "The bicycle!"

With that, a long flexible grappel emerged from the pit and seized the vehicle's frame just beneath the seat. It raised it from the ground and drew it toward the shaft. Pete caught at the handlebars as it passed by, digging in with his heels and pulling back on it.

"Let go of my bike! Damn it! I just want some information!"

It wrenched it away from him and drew it down into the opening.

"Customer to stand by for maintenance and repairs!" it shouted.

The arm emerged again and deposited a red-vinyl-and-tube-aluminum chair, a rack of *Readers' Digest*s, a stand ashtray, and a section of pale green partitioning on which was hung a *Playboy* calendar, a faded and fly-specked print of Crater Lake, and signs saying THE CUSTOMER IS ALWAYS RIGHT; SMILE; THIMK; I DON'T GET

ULCERS. I GIVE THEM; and ONLY YOU CAN PREVENT FOREST FIRES.

Sighing, Pete seated himself and began reading an article on the cure for cancer.

A humming noise arose from deep in the pit, rapidly growing into a roar, accompanied by an irregular banging and the screeches of tearing metal. Moments later, he heard the lift grinding its way upward.

"Service with maximum efficiency!" the voice brayed. "Stand by to receive product!"

Pete rose and retreated from the shaft opening. Three arms were then extended in rapid succession. Each of them clutched a shiny tricycle.

"God damn it!" he cried. "You ruined my bike!"

The arms hesitated, halted.

"The customer is not satisfied?" a soft, lethal voice inquired.

"Well—they are beautiful tricycles," he said. "Real quality workmanship. Anyone can see that. It is just that I needed only one, full-size—and with two wheels, one front and one rear."

"All right. Stand by for adjustment!"

"While you are about it," Pete said, "could you tell me what occurred when Tibor McMasters came here?"

The tricycles were withdrawn and the noises began again. Above them, the voice roared out, "The little phoc left me an order and didn't come back for it or the abortion. Here!" A carton of lube was expelled from the opening and landed near his feet. "That's his order! Give it to him yourself if you want—and tell him I don't need people like him for customers!"

Pete snatched up the carton and continued to back away, as the noises under the ground had grown to an ominous, thunderlike level, so that now the earth began to tremble from their vibration.

"*Your order is now ready!*" it rumbled. "*Stand by!*"

Pete turned and ran, crashing back through the thicket.

A shadow darkened the heavens, and he threw himself into the lea of a boulder and covered his head with his hands.

It began to rain pogo sticks.

FOURTEEN

Tibor watched the evening change clothes about him,
saw the landscape divide and depart, up and down,
dark. How did it go, that desolate little poem? It was
Rilke's "Abend":

> Der Abend wechselt langsam die Gewänder,
> die ihm Rand von alten Bäumen hält;
> du schaust: und von dir scheiden sich die Länder,
> ein himmelfahrendes und eins, das fällt;
>
> und lassen dich, zu keinem ganz gehörend,
> nicht ganz so dunkel wie das Haus, das schweigt,
> nicht ganz so sicher Ewiges beschwörend
> wie das, was Stern wird jede Nacht und steigt;
>
> und lassen die (unsäglich zu entwirrn)
> dein Leben, bang und riesenhaft und reifend,
> so dasz es, bald begrenzt und bald begreifend,
> abwechselnd Stein in dir wird und Gestirn.

He knows how I feel, he decided, to none belonging,
not so surely promised to eternity as all this, confused,
alone, afraid. If I could turn to stone and stars now, I
would. The God of Wrath gave me legs and arms. He
took them back again. Did that really happen? Yes, it
did. I'm sure of it. Why did he give me limbs if I

couldn't keep them? Just to hold anything and feel it for a time would be so fine. I thought it was sadistic, but the Christian version is a masochist now that I think of it, a turning upon oneself of all bad things, which is just as bad in its own way. He loves everybody, democratically, in fact relentlessly. But he created people so that they could not go through life without hurting him. He wanted something painful to love. They're both of them sick. They have to be. —How horrible I feel, how worthless. But I still don't want to die. I am afraid to use the bullhorn again, though. Now that it is dark. No telling what might hear it and come—now.

Tibor began to weep. The night sounds—chirps, buzzes, the dry rasping of twigs on bark—were smothered by his sobs.

There came a jolt and a creak, as an extra weight was added to his cart. Oh god! What's that? he thought. I am totally helpless. I will have to lie here and let it eat me. It is too dark to see where I could even direct the extensor to defend myself. It's somewhere behind me, advancing now—

He felt a cold, moist touch upon his neck, then fur. It came up beside him. It licked his cheek.

"Toby! Toby . . ."

It was the dog the lizards had given him. It had run off earlier, and he had assumed it was on its way back to its former owners. Now he saw the muzzle outlined against the sky, tongue rolling, teeth white, approximating a smile.

"You've stayed with me after all," he said. "I don't have anything to feed you. I hope you found something yourself. Stay with me. Curl up and sleep here beside me. Please. I'll keep talking to you, Toby. Good dog, good dog . . . Sorry I can't pet you. In this light, I might misjudge and crush your skull. Stay, though. Stay . . ."

If I make it through the night, he thought . . . *if I make it it'll be because of you.*

"I'll reward you someday," he promised the dog, who stirred at the emphatic tone of his voice. "I will save your life. If you save mine, if I am alive when help comes—I promise! If I am still living when yourself are ever in danger, you will hear a roaring and a rushing, and a rolling, and the brush will churn! Leaves and dust will fly up, and you will know I am on my way, from wherever I am, to aid you! The thunder and violent rolling of my salvation of you will terrify anyone. I will protect you, cherish you, exactly as you are getting me through this night tonight. That is my sacred solemn promise before God Himself."

The dog thumped his tail.

Pete Sands, walking under the moon, across the nighted plain, hiking between the tracks of the cow cart, pausing periodically to assure himself they remain: Shouldn't be abroad after dark. Should find some sheltered place and bed down. Want more distance between me and that schizy autofac, though. Guess I've probably come far enough. But now I feel vulnerable, exposed. Flat, empty, this place. But there were trees in the distance when the light went away. This still seems the proper direction. That right track is getting wobbly. Without the lube, that tire could go. Is he all right? My hip is sore. Lost my hat, too. Now my head will turn red and peel. Then red again. Then peel again. It never tans over. . . . How *is* Tibor faring? How strong are those manual grippers? I wonder. Could he protect himself? My knee hurts, too. There's one problem he'll never have. Life would be so much simpler if Lufteufel had had the decency to die back when he should have and everybody knew it. Now, though . . . What will I do if he really turns up? Supposing he pets dogs and gives candy to children these days? Supposing he has a wife and ten kids who love him? Supposing . . . Hell! Too much supposing. What would Lurine say? I don't know what Lurine would say. . . . Where'd that damn track go?

He squatted and searched the ground. It had become gravelly, digesting the ruts. Rising again, he shrugged and continued on. No reason to assume a sudden change of direction. Continue in a straight line for now.

He reinspected the trail periodically, but it retained a coarse, stony texture. I'll have to search it out in the morning, he decided.

Trudging ahead, he noted a faint flickering off to his left, just becoming apparent about the edge of a cluster of stones. Moving farther, more of the light reached him, finally revealing itself as a small campfire. Only one figure was outlined in its vicinity, a being with a strangely pointed head. It was kneeling, its attention apparently focused on the flames.

Pete slowed, studying the tableau. Moments later, the breeze brought him a tangy odor and his mouth grew moist. It had been a long while since last he had eaten.

He stood but a moment longer, then turned and made his way toward the fire, moving slowly, cautiously. As he drew nearer, he caught a glint of the light on a metal headpiece. It was a spiked helmet, of a sort he was not likely to forget too readily. Then he glimpsed the features below it. Yes, no mistake there.

He moved ahead quickly then.

"Hunter!" he said. "You *are* the same man. Aren't you? Back at the Great C's—"

The man laughed, three deep-chested explosions that shook the flames he tended.

"Yes, yes! Come and sit down! I hate to eat alone."

Pete dropped his pack and hunkered beside it, across the fire from the man.

"I'd've sworn you were dead," he said. "All that blood. You were limp. I thought it had killed you. Then when it dragged you inside . . . I was sure you were gone."

The man nodded, turning the little spits of bone on which chunks of meat were skewered.

"I can see how you might have been misled," he said. "Here!"

The man drew a kabob from the fire and passed it to him. Pete licked his fingers for insulation and accepted it. The meat was good, juicy. Pete debated asking what it was, and decided against it. A hunter can always find something edible. Best to leave it at that.

The man ate with an unnatural precision, and Pete could see the reason as he studied his face: his lower lip had been badly cut, split deeply.

"Yes," the man muttered, "the blood could have been deceiving—part from my mouth and part from a recent head wound that reopened. That's why I was wearing the armor." He tapped the headpiece. "Good thing, too. Kept it from pulping my skull."

"But how," Pete said, "did you get away from it?"

"Oh. No real problem," he replied. "I came out of it just as it dragged me inside. I'd already loosened the cranial bolt to the springing point. One twist was what I said and one twist was what it took. With my fingers. Presto!" He snapped his fingers. He popped another piece of meat into his mouth. "Then it was down and I was up and that was it. Pity. But then, I'd given it every break. You know that, don't you?"

"You were most fair with it," Pete said, finishing his kabob and eyeing the others that still sizzled.

The man passed him another.

And his hands are still steady, Pete thought, accepting the meat. All in a day's work. Competency, expertise—nerves like fine-spun filaments of platinum, joints like neatly mashed gears and stainless-steel ball bearings. Skill, guts—that's what it takes to be a hunter. But he's got heart, too. Compassion. How many of us would be that concerned over something that wanted to devour us?

"After I left that place," the hunter said, "I continued on my way, pleased to see that you had had the good sense to clear out."

Oh my god! Pete thought. I hope he was really unconscious, not just saying that. What if he heard me asking the C to take him instead of me? But then, I really thought he was dead. I just told him so. So even if he did hear me say it, he'd know that that was why. But I could have told him that now, just to look good, even though it wasn't what I had in mind when I said it. On the other hand, if he heard it he must be a big enough man to have forgiven me—in which case he is pretending he didn't hear it—which means that I will never know. Oh my god! And here I am eating his kabobs.

"What became of your bike?" the hunter asked him.

"The autofac turned it into pogo sticks," Pete said. The hunter smiled.

"Not surprising," he said. "Once their naderers go, they do the damnedest things. But you were carrying something you didn't have before. Did it actually fill an order properly before it ruined your bike?"

"Someone else's order," Pete said. "Its delivery sequence is off, too."

"What are you going to do with all that lube?"

"I am taking it to a man who probably needs it," Pete said, recalling the C's statement that the hunter was after Tibor. Easily a piece of misinformation. Still . . .

He stuffed his mouth to avoid answering anything

further without at least a ten-second pause for thought.

Why would he be looking for Tibor, though? he wondered. What could he want of him? What would make Tibor worth hunting? To anyone else, that is . . . ?

When they finished eating, Pete knew that he should offer the man one of his remaining cigarettes. He did so, and he took one for himself. They lit them with a brand from the fire and sprawled then near the boulders, resting, smoking.

"I don't know," Pete said, "about the propriety of the question. So please excuse me if I am being impolite. I don't meet so many hunters that I am up on the etiquette. I was just wondering: Are you hunting anything or anyone in particular just now, or are you—between hunts?"

"Oh, I'm on a hunt all right," the man said. "I'm looking for a little phocomelus named Tibor McMasters. I think the trail is fairly warm now, too."

"Oh, really?" said Pete, drawing on his cigarette, one hand beneath his head, his eyes on the stars. "What did he do?"

"Oh, nothing, nothing yet. He is not especially important. Just part of a bigger design."

"Oh." Now what do I say? he wondered. Then, "By the way, my name is Pete. Pete Sands."

"I know."

"I forgot to introduce myself earlier, and— You know? How could you?"

"Because I know of everyone in Charlottesville, Utah—everyone with any connection with Tibor McMasters, that is. It's a small town. There aren't that many of you."

"Efficient," Pete said, feeling as if barbs inserted painlessly into his flesh were now being drawn. "Your employer must have gone to a lot of trouble and expense. It would have been easier to approach the man back in town."

"But fruitless, there," the other replied. "And the difficulty and the cost mean nothing to my employer."

Pete waited, smoking. He felt positive that it would be a breach of etiquette to inquire as to his employer's identity. *Perhaps if I just wait he will volunteer it,* he decided.

The fire crackled. In the distance, something howled and something else chuckled.

"My name is Schuld, Jack Schuld," the hunter said, extending his hand.

Pete turned onto his side and clasped it. The grip was, as he suspected, powerful enough to crush his own, while sufficiently controlled to show this without exerting considerable force. Releasing it, Pete leaned back and contemplated stellar geometries. A meteor smeared white fire across the sky. *When the stars threw down their spears,* he remembered, *And water'd heaven with their tears* . . . What came next? He could not recall.

"Tibor is on a dangerous Pilg," Schuld said, "and he has recently expressed a desire to convert to the religion wherein you would take your ministry."

"You are indeed thorough," Pete observed.

"Yes, I'd say so. You Christians aren't doing so well these days," he continued, "and even a single convert comes to mean a lot in a little place like Charlottesville, Utah. Right?"

"I can't deny it," Pete said.

"So your superior has sent you to take care of the catechumen, to see that he comes to no harm while finishing his job for the competition."

"I do want to find him and protect him," Pete said.

"And the subject of his search? Have you any curiosity concerning the one he has been commissioned to portray?"

"Oh, I sometimes wonder whether the man is still really living," Pete said.

"Man?" Schuld said. "You can still call him that?"

"Well, unlike our competitors, I do not really see him as fitted for any larger role."

"I was not talking theology," Schuld said. "I was simply noting your reference to humanity when speaking of one who has forfeited all right to any human considerations. Adolph Eichmann was an altar boy by comparison. We are speaking of the beast who destroyed most of the world."

"I cannot deny the act, but neither can I judge it. How can I know his motives, his intent?"

"Look around you. Anytime. Anywhere. Their effects are manifest in every phase of existence now. He is, to put it bluntly and concisely, an inhuman monster."

Pete nodded.

"Maybe," he said. "If he truly understood the nature and quality of his actions, then I suppose he was something unspeakable at the time."

"Try Carleton Lufteufel. It can be spoken. There is not a living creature on Earth today that has not known pain because of him. There is nothing to which he does not owe a sea of misery, a continent of despair. He has been marked from the day he made his decision."

"I had heard that hunters were mercenaries, that they do not act out of conviction."

"You anticipate me, Pete. I have not named him as my quarry."

Pete chuckled. So did Schuld.

"But they are fortunate times, when desire and circumstance are conjoined," Schuld finally said.

"Then why do you seek Tibor?" Pete asked. "I do not quite understand the connection."

"The beast is wary," the other replied, "but I doubt his suspicions would extend to a phocomelus."

"I begin to see."

"Yes. I will lead him to him. Tibor can have his likeness. I will have his flesh."

Pete shuddered. The situation had twisted and darkened, but might, for all that, be turning to his advantage.

"Are you planning to make a quick, clean thing of it?" he asked.

"No," Schuld replied. "I am charged to make certain that it is just the opposite. I am, you see, employed by a worldwide secret police organization which has been searching for Lufteufel for years—for just this purpose."

"I understand," Pete said. "I can almost wish that I did not know this. Almost . . ."

"I am telling you this because it will make it easier for me if one of you knows. As for Tibor, he has been a member of the Servants of Wrath, and its symbols may still have some hold over him. You, on the other hand, represent the opposing camp. Do you see what I mean?"

"You mean, will I cooperate?"

"Yes. Will you?"

"I do not think myself capable of stopping a person such as you."

"That is not what I asked."

"I know." Damn it! I wish I could talk to Abernathy right now, he thought. But there is no way to get off the call. But he would not give me a real answer. I have to decide this one for myself. Tibor must not be permitted to meet Lufteufel. There ought to be a way. I will have time to find a way—and then let Schuld do the job for me. There is nothing else for me to say now, but, "All right, Jack. I'll cooperate."

"Good," Schuld replied. "I knew that you would."

He felt that powerful hand clasp his shoulder for an instant. In that same instant he felt hemmed in by the stone and the stars.

FIFTEEN

Into the world, the day, spilling: here: the queries of birds, tentative, then self-assured: here: dew like breath on glass, retreating, gone: here: bands of color that flee the east, fading, fading, blue: here: like a wax doll, half melted: Tibor, soft in the collapsed cart; cock-eared hound by his side, watching the world come around.

A yawn then, a blinking, slow memory. Tibor bunched and relaxed his shoulder muscles. Isometrics. Stretching. Bunching. Relaxing.

"Good morning, Toby. Another day. This one will tell it, I guess. You *are* a good dog. Damn good. Best dog I ever knew. You can get down now. Hunt up breakfast if you know how. It's the only way you'll get any, I'm afraid."

Toby jumped down, relieved himself beside a tree, circled the cart, sniffed the ground. Tibor activated the extensor and proceeded with his own simple ablutions.

I suppose I should try the bullhorn again, now, he thought. But I am afraid to. I really am. It is my last hope. If it fails me, nothing else remains.

He hesitated a long while. He searched the sky, the trees.

The blue jay? Is that what I am looking for? he wondered. I don't know what I am looking for. I guess that I am not truly awake yet. There goes Toby into the brush. I wonder if I will ever see him again? I may be dead by the time he gets back. No telling what— Stop it! Okay. A cup of coffee would be nice. It would be so nice. A last cup . . . All right! I'll try the horn.

He raised it, turned it on, and called out:

"Hallo! This is Tibor McMasters. I have had an accident. My cart is stuck. I am caught here. If anyone can hear me, I need help. Can you hear me? Can you help me? Is anyone there?"

Nothing. He waited for perhaps fifteen minutes and tried again. Again nothing.

Three more attempts. An hour drawn and quartered. Toby returned, discussed something with the cow, lay down in the shade.

Faintly . . . Was that a shout? Or a tricking of the ear? A thing compounded of hope, fear, background sounds? The cry of an animal?

He began to perspire, straining to hear through the natural noises, listening for it to come again.

Toby whined.

Turning, Tibor saw that the dog had risen to its feet and was facing back along the trail, ears pointed, body tense.

He switched on the horn and raised it once again.

"Hallo! Hallo! Over here! Up here! I am trapped! Caught in a collapsed cart! This is Tibor McMasters! I have had an accident! Can you hear me?"

"Yes!" The word echoed among the hills. "We are coming!"

Tibor began to laugh. His eyes were moist. He chuckled. At that moment, he thought he glimpsed the blue jay darting away among the trees. But he could not be certain.

"We are going to finish this Pilg yet, Toby," he said. "We are going to make it, I think."

It was another ten minutes before Pete Sands and Jack Schuld rounded the bend of the trail and came into view. Toby laid his ears flat and growled, backing up against the cart.

"It's all right, Toby," Tibor said. "I know one of them. He is here to do the Christian thing. Be a handy samaritan and look over my shoulder afterward. And I need him. The price is right, whatever."

"Tibor!" Pete called out. "Are you hurt?"

"No, it's just the cart," he answered. "Threw a wheel."

They approached.

"I see the wheel," Pete said. He glanced at his companion. "This is Jack Schuld. I met him on the trail yesterday. This is Tibor McMasters, Jack—a great artist."

Tibor nodded.

"I can't shake hands," he said.

Schuld smiled.

"I'll lend you mine," he said. "We'll have that wheel back on in no time. Pete has some lube."

Schuld crossed to the wheel, raised it from the brush where it had come to rest, rolled it toward the cart.

Nimble, Tibor thought. All connoisseurs of the movements of the unmaimed would probably agree on that. What does he want?

Toby snarled as Schuld brought the wheel around to the front of the cart.

"Back up, Toby! Go away now! They're helping me," Tibor said.

The dog slunk off a dozen paces and sat down, watching.

Pete brought the lube around.

"We're going to have to raise the cart," he said. "I wonder . . . ?"

"I'll raise it," Schuld said.

As they worked, Tibor said, "I suppose I should ask what you are doing out this way."

Pete looked up and smiled. Then he sighed.

"You know," he said. "You left early because you didn't want me along. All right. But I had to follow— just because of the possibility of things like this." He gestured at the cart.

"All right," Tibor said. "All right. As it turns out, I am not ungrateful. Thanks for showing up."

"May I take that as an indication that I will be welcome for the balance of the journey?"

Tibor chuckled.

"Let's just say that I can't object to your presence now."

"I guess that will have to do."

Pete turned his attention back to the work.

"Where did you meet Mr. Schuld?"

"He saved me in an encounter with the Great C's extension."

"Handy," Tibor said.

Schuld laughed and Tibor was jolted as the man crouched beneath the cart, then stood, raising it on his shoulders.

"Jack Schuld *is* handy," he said. "Yes, he is," and, "Indeed. —Fit it on over the hub now, Pete."

I suppose that I should feel happy to have people around me again, thought Tibor, after everything I have encountered recently. Still . . .

"There," Pete said. "You can lower it now."

Schuld eased the cart down, moved out from beneath it. Pete began tightening a nut.

"I am much obliged," Tibor said.

"Think nothing of it," Schuld replied. "Glad to be of help. —Your friend tells me you are on a Pilg."

"That's right. Part of a commission I have—"

"Yes, he told me about that, too. Off to get a glimpse of old Lufteufel for your mural. Worthy project, I'd say. And I believe you are getting warm."

"You know something about him?"

"I think so. There have been rumors, you know. I travel a lot. I hear them all. Some say that's his town to the north. —No, you can't see it from here. But keep going this way and you'll eventually come to a settlement. That's the one—they say."

"Do you believe the rumors?"

Schuld rubbed his dark chin and a faraway look came into his eyes.

"I would think the odds are pretty good," he said. "Yes. I fancy I could find him there."

"I don't suppose he uses his real name anymore," Tibor said. "He has probably assumed a different identity."

Schuld nodded.

"I understand that to be the case."

"Do you know it?"

"The name? No. The identity? I think so. I have heard that he is a veterinarian now, that he makes his home in a remodeled fallout shelter, has a feebleminded girl living there with him."

"Is this place in the town proper?"

"No. Out a ways from town. Easy to miss—they say."

Pete sighed and stood. He plucked a bunch of leaves and began wiping his hands. He finished the job on his trousers.

"There," he said. "Now if we push and you can make the cow pull, we should be able to get it back on the trail. Then we can see how it holds up. —Give me a hand now, Jack, will you?"

Schuld moved away, circling to the rear of the cart.

"All right, ready," Pete said.

"Ready."

"Push!"

"Giddap!" Tibor said.

The cart creaked, rocked forward, back, forward, forward, continued on along the ditch, caught the incline, rose with it. A minute later, they had it back on the trail.

"Try it now," Pete said. "See how it moves on the level."

Tibor set out.

"Better," he said. "I can feel the difference. Much better."

"Good."

They continued on along the trail then, up, down, around, about the hills.

"How far are you going?" Tibor asked Schuld.

"A good distance," the man replied. "I am going through that town we spoke of. We might as well go that far together."

"Yes. Do you think you might have time to point that place out to me?"

"Lufteufel's? Surely. I'll try. I'll show you where I think it is. You see, I want to help."

"Well, that would be very helpful," Tibor said. "When do you think we will reach it?"

"Perhaps sometime tomorrow."

Tibor nodded.

"What do you really think about him?" he asked.

"A good question," the hunter replied, "and one I knew you would get to sooner or later. What do I think of him?" He pulled his nose. He ran his fingers through his hair. "I have traveled widely," he said, "and I have seen much of the world, both before and after. I lived through the days of the destruction. I saw the cities die, the countryside wilt. I saw the pallor come upon the land. There was still some beauty in the old days, you know. The cities were hectic, dirty places, but at certain moments—usually times of arrival and departure— looking down upon them at night, all lit up, say, from a plane in a cloudless sky—you could almost, for that moment, call up a vision out of St. Augustine. *Urbi et orbi,* perhaps, for that clear instant. And once you got away from the towns, on a good day, there was a lot of green and brown, sprinkled with all the other colors, clear running water, sweet air— But the day came. The wrath descended. Sin, guilt, and retribution? The manic psychoses of those entities we referred to as states, institutions, systems—the powers, the thrones, the dominations—the things which perpetually merge with men and emerge from them? Our darkness, externalized and visible? However you look upon these matters, the critical point was reached. The wrath descended. The good, the evil, the beautiful, the dark, the cities, the country— the entire world—all were mirrored for an instant within the upraised blade. The hand that held that blade was Carleton Lufteufel's. In the moment that it plunged toward our heart, it was no longer the hand of a man, but that of the Deus Irae, the God of Wrath Himself. That which remains exists by virtue of His sufferance. If there is to be any religion at all, I see this as the only tenable credo. What other construction could be placed upon the events? That is how I see Carleton Lufteufel, how I feel he must be preserved in your art. That is why I am willing to point him out for you."

"I see," said Tibor, waiting for Pete's reaction, disappointed when none was forthcoming. Then, "It does make sense," he said, partly to irritate Pete. "The greatest painters of the Renaissance had a go at depicting the other. But none of them actually got to see their subject, to glimpse the visage of God. I am going to do it, and when men look upon that painting they will know that I have, for it will be true. They will say, 'Tibor McMasters has seen, and he has shown what he saw.' "

Schuld slapped the side of the cart and chuckled.

"Soon," he said. "Soon."

* * *

That evening, as they were gathering kindling for a campfire, Pete said to Schuld, "You took him in entirely, I'd say. That business about wanting to see Lufteufel preserved in his art, I mean."

"Pride," Schuld replied. "It was easy. Got his mind off me and onto himself quickly. Now I am a part of his Pilg: Guide. I will speak to him again later this evening, confidentially. Perhaps if you were to take a brief walk after dinner . . ."

"Of course."

"When I have finished, any second thoughts he may have had as to my sincerity will be laid to rest. Everything should proceed smoothly afterward."

The subtlety and sense of timing of a thermostat or a cardiac pacemaker, Pete decided—that's what it takes to be a hunter—a feeling for the rhythm of things and a power over them. This is going well. Only Tibor must *not* really see Lufteufel. . . .

"I believe you," Pete said. Then, "I don't quite know how to put this, though, so I will simply be direct: Do either of the two religions involved in this mean anything to you personally?"

A huge stick snapped between Schuld's hands.

"No," he said.

"I didn't think so, but I wanted to clear that up first. As you know, one of them means something to me."

"Obviously."

"What I am getting at is the fact that we Christians would not be overjoyed at seeing Lufteufel actually represented in that mural."

"A false religion, a false god, as you would have it. What difference does it make what they stick in their church?"

"Power," Pete said. "You can appreciate that. From a strictly temporal standpoint, having the real thing—as they see it—would give them something more. Call it mana. If we suddenly had a piece of the True Cross, it would whip up our zeal a bit, put a little more fire into our activities. You must be familiar with the phenomenon. Call it inspiration."

Schuld laughed.

"Whatever Tibor paints, they will believe it is the real thing. The results will be the same."

He wants me to say that I believe in the God of Wrath and am afraid of him, Pete thought. I won't do it.

"Such being the case, we would as soon it were not Lufteufel," Pete said.

"Why?"

"Because we would look on *that* as blasphemy, as a mockery of God as we see Him. They would be deifying not just any man, but the man responsible for all our present woes, the man you yourself referred to as an inhuman monster."

Schuld snapped another stick.

"Yes, of course," he said. "He doesn't deserve a neatly dug hole in the ground, let alone worship. I see your point. What do you propose doing?"

"Use us for your cover," Pete said, "as you had planned. Locate him. Get as close as you feel necessary to satisfy yourself as to his identity. Then tell Tibor you were mistaken. He is *not* the man. Our ways part there. We go on, continuing our search. You remain behind or depart and double back—whichever is easier—and do what you must do. Lufteufel is thus removed from our field of consideration."

"What will you do then?"

"I don't know. Keep going. Maybe locate a substitute. I don't know. But at least Carleton Lufteufel will be out of the picture."

"That, then, is your real reason for being here? Not just the protection of Tibor?"

"It might have figured in the decision—a little."

Schuld laughed again.

"How far were you willing to go to insure Tibor's not seeing him? I wonder. Might it extend to actual violence?"

Pete snapped a stick of his own.

"You said it," he said. "I didn't."

"I may be doing you people a favor just by doing my job," Schuld said.

"Maybe."

"Too bad I didn't know about it sooner. If a man is going to labor for two masters, he might as well draw good wages from both of them."

"Christianity is broke," Pete said. "But I'll remember you in my prayers."

Schuld slapped him on the shoulder.

"Pete, I like you," he said. "Okay. We'll do it your way. Tibor doesn't have to know."

"Thanks."

Beneath that Swiss movement, Pete wondered as they headed back, what is the spark—the mainspring— really like, hunter? The money they will pay you? The hate? Or something else?

There came a sharp yelp. Schuld had kicked Toby, who had emerged before him, snarling. It could have been an accident, but, "Damn dog!" he said. "It hates me."

SIXTEEN

Pete Sands set up his radio gear by moonlight, working in the middle of a small glade about a quarter of a mile back along the road from the site of their encampment.

Neat, he thought, the way it worked out, Schuld's suggesting what I was going to do anyway: take this walk.

He plugged in the earphone, cranked the transmitter.

"Dr. Abernathy," he said, raising the microphone. "Pete Sands here. Hello?"

There followed a brief burst of static, then, "Hello, Pete. This is Abernathy. How is it going?"

"I've located Tibor," Pete said.

"Is he aware of your presence?"

"Yes. We are traveling together now. I am calling from just outside our camp."

"Oh. So you have joined him. What are your plans?"

"They are somewhat complicated," Pete said. "There is a third party involved—a fellow named Jack Schuld. I met him yesterday. He saved my life, actually. He seems to have a pretty good idea as to Lufteufel's whereabouts. He has offered to guide us to him. We may reach the place tomorrow."

Pete smiled at the sharp intake of breath on the other end. He continued: "I have made a deal with him, however. He will not point him out to Tibor. He is going to confess to a case of mistaken identity and we will bypass the real Lufteufel and continue on."

"Wait a minute, Pete. I do not understand you. Why go through all that in the first place then? Why go that route at all?"

"Well," Pete said lamely, "he will do me this favor in return for our company on the way."

"Pete, what are you leaving out? It doesn't make sense. There has to be more to it than that."

"All right. He is an assassin. He is on his way to kill Lufteufel. He thinks he would seem less suspicious traveling in the company of an inc."

"Pete! That makes you a party to murder!"

"Not really. I disapprove of murder. We discussed that earlier. And he may even have a legal right to do this—as an executioner. He *is* in the employ of a police organization—at least he says he is, and I believe him. Whatever, I am powerless to stop him, no matter what my feelings. If you got a good look at him, you would know what I mean. I thought you would be happy to learn—"

"—of a man's death. Pete, I don't like this at all."

"Then suggest something else, sir."

"Could you get away from this Schuld? You and Tibor sneak off during the night? Just go on by yourselves?"

"Too late. Tibor would not cooperate if I couldn't give him an awfully good reason—and I can't. He believes Schuld can show him his man. And I am certain we could not sneak off anyway. Schuld is too alert a fellow. He's a hunter."

"Do you think you could warn Lufteufel when you reach him?"

"No," Pete said, "not now that I've set it up for Tibor to miss him completely or only to glimpse him without knowing who he is. —I didn't think you would take it this way."

"I am trying to protect you from an occasion for sin."

"I don't see it as such."

". . . Most likely mortal."

"I hope not. I guess that I am going to have to play it by ear now. I will let you know what happens."

"Wait, Pete! Listen! Try to find some way to part company with that Schuld fellow as fast as possible. If it weren't for him, you wouldn't even be going near Lufteufel. You are not responsible for Schuld's actions unless you are in a position to influence them by action or the withholding of action yourself. Morally as well as practically, you are better off without him. Get out! Get away from him!"

"And leave Tibor?"

"No, take Tibor with you."

"Against his will? Kidnap him, you mean?"

There was silence, then a little static.

Finally, "I don't know how to tell you to do it," he said. "That is your problem. But you must look for a way."

"I will see what I can do," Pete said, "but it doesn't look promising."

"I will continue to pray," Dr. Abernathy replied. "When will you call me again?"

"Tomorrow evening, I guess. I probably won't be able to get off a call during the day."

"All right. I will be waiting. Good night."

"Good night."

The static gave way to crickets. Pete disassembled the gear.

"Tibor," Schuld said, stirring the fire, "Tibor McMasters, on his way to immortality."

"Huh?" said Tibor. He had been staring into the

flames, finding the face of a girl named Fay Blaine who had been more than kind to him in the past. If He had left me those arms and legs, he had been thinking, I could go back and tell her how I really feel. I could hold her, run my fingers through her hair, mold her form like a sculptor. She would let me, too, I think. I would be like other men. I . . .

"Huh?"

"Immortality," Schuld repeated. "Better than progeny, even, for they have a way of disappointing, embarrassing, hurting their begetters. But painting is 'the grandchild of nature and related to God.' "

"I do not understand," Tibor said.

" 'Though the poet is as free as the painter in the invention of his fictions, they are not so satisfactory to men as paintings,' " Schuld said, " 'for, though poetry is able to describe forms, actions, and places in words, the painter deals with the actual similitude of the forms, in order to represent them. Now tell me which is the nearer to the actual man: the name of the man or the image of the man. The name of the man differs in different countries, but his form is never changed but by death.' "

"I think I see what you mean," Tibor said.

" '. . . And this is true knowledge and the legitimate issue of nature.' Leonardo da Vinci wrote that in one of his notebooks. It feels right, too. And it will fit the present case so well. You will be remembered, Tibor McMasters, not for a passel of snot-nosed brats creeping toward eternity's rim, dull variations on the DNA you're stuck with, but for the exercise of your power to create the other image—the deathless similitude of a particular form. And you will be father to a vision that rises above nature itself, that is superior to it because divine. Among all men, you have been singled out for this measure of immortality."

Tibor smiled.

"It is quite a responsibility they've given me," he said.

"You are very modest," Schuld said, "and more than a little naïve. Do you think you were chosen simply because you were the best painter in town when the SOWs needed a murch? There is more to it than that. Would you believe that Charlottesville, Utah, was chosen to house the murch before it was *your* town? Would you believe that your town was chosen because you are the greatest artist alive today?"

Tibor turned and stared at him.

"Father Handy never indicated anything like that," he said.

"He gets his orders, as do those from whom he takes them."

"You have lost me—again," Tibor said. "How could you know these things?"

Schuld smiled and stared at him, head tilted upward, eyes half lidded, his face almost pulsing in the flamelight.

"Because I gave the first order," he said. "I wanted you for my artist. I am the head of the Servants of Wrath, the temporal leader of the true religion of the Deus Irae."

"My God!" said Tibor.

"Yes," said Schuld. "For obvious reasons, I waited until now to tell you. I was not about to proclaim myself in front of Pete Sands."

"Is Schuld your real name?" Tibor asked him.

"The name of a man differs in different countries. Schuld will do. I joined you at this point in your Pilg because I intend personally to see that you find the proper man. Pete will doubtless try to misdirect you. He has his orders, of course. But I will see to it that you are not misled. I will name Lufteufel, give you his form at the proper time. Nothing the Old Church can do will prevent it. I want you to be aware of this."

"I felt there was something unusual about you," Tibor said. Indeed I did, he thought. But not this. I know little of the hierarchical setup of the Servants of Wrath. Just that there is one. I had always assumed the murch represented a local decision in terms of interior decoration. It does make sense, though, when you think about it. Lufteufel is at the center of the religion. Anything involving him personally would warrant attention at the highest levels. And this man Schuld is the boss. If he were going to appear at all, this is the perfect time. No one else could have known, would have known, could have come up with that reason or effected this timing. I believe him.

"I believe you," Tibor said. "And it is somewhat—overwhelming. Thank you for your confidence in me. I will try to be worthy of it."

"You are," Schuld said, "which is why you were chosen. And I will tell you now that it may be a sudden thing, that I may have to arrange the encounter quite unexpectedly. Pete's presence requires this. You must be prepared at any time from now on to record what I indicate, at a moment's notice."

"I will keep my camera ready," Tibor said, activating his extensor and moving the device into a new position, "and my eyes, of course—they are always ready."

"Good. That is all that I really require, for now. Once you have captured the image, neither Pete nor his entire church can take it away from you. The murch will proceed, as planned."

"Thank you," said Tibor. "You have made me happy. I hope that Pete does not interfere—"

Schuld rose and squeezed his shoulder.

"I like you," he said. "Have no fear. I have planned everything."

Stowing his gear, Pete Sands thought of Dr. Abernathy's words, and he thought of Schuld, and of Carleton Lufteufel.

He cannot come out and tell me to kill Lufteufel, even though he knows that would solve our problem. He cannot even disregard Schuld's intention in this direction, once he has heard of it. It is a damnable dilemma which cleaves all the way back to the basic paradox involved in loving everyone, even the carnifex about to poleax you. Logically, if you do nothing you die and he has his way. If you are the only one practicing such a philosophy, it dies with you. A few others—all right—he gets them, too, and it still dies. The noble ideal, *caritas,* passes from the world. If we kill to prevent this, though, we betray it. It gets Zen-like here: Do nothing and the destroyer moves. Do something and you destroy it yourself. Yet you are charged to preserve it. How? The answer is supposed to be that it is a divine law and will win out anyhow. I crack the *koan* simultaneously with an act of giving up on it. Then I am granted insight into its meaning. Or, in Christian terms, my will is empowered upon an especially trying occasion and I am granted an extraordinary measure of grace. I don't feel any of it flowing this way at the moment, though. In fact, I begin to feel that I am beating my brains out against an impossible situation. I don't want to kill Lufteufel, really. I don't want to kill anybody. My reasons are not theological. They are just simple humanitarian things. I don't like to cause pain. It may well be that if that poor bastard is still living, he has done a lot of suffering on his own already. I don't know. I don't care to know. Also, I'm squeamish.

Pete hefted his pack and moved on out of the glade.

With this, he thought as he walked, where is that *caritas* I am supposed to be practicing? Not too much of that around either. Can I love Carleton Lufteufel—or anyone—on such a plane that what they are, what they have done, counts for nothing? Where only the fact of existence is sufficient qualification as target for the arrow of this feeling? This would indeed be God-like, and is, I suppose, the essence of the ideal that we should strive to emulate the greater love. I don't know. There have been occasions when I have felt that way, however briefly. What lay at their heart? Biochemistry, perhaps. Looking for ultimate causes is really an impossible quest. I remember that day, though, with Lurine. "What's *ein Todesstachel?*" she had asked, and I told her of the sting of death and then oh God had felt it coming into my side piercing like a metal gaff twisting hooking oh Lord driving my body to an agonized *Totentanz* about the room Lurine trying to restrain me and up then looking along the pole from Earth to heaven ascending to the Persons then three who held me and into the eyes that saw oh Lurine the heart of my quest and your question there here and everywhere the pain never to cease and piercing the joy that is beyond and quickens as it slays again in the heart of the wood and the night oh Everyone I am here I did not ask to but I did—

Ahead, he could make out the forms of Schuld and Tibor in the firelight. They were laughing, they seemed to be happy and that should be good. He felt something brush against his leg. Looking down, he saw that it was Toby. He reached out to pat the upturned head.

Alice held the doll, crooning to it, swaying. She rocked back and forth from one foot to the other. The corridor slanted gently before her. Squatting, she placed the doll on the truck. With a small push, she started it on its journey down the tunnel. She laughed as it sped away. When it struck the wall and turned over, she screamed.

"No! No! No! No!"

Running to it, she raised the doll and held it.

"No," she said. "Be all right."

She set the truck upright, reinstalled the doll.

"Now!" she said, pushing it again.

Her laughter followed it as it spun on its way, avoiding the obstacles which had collected in the corridor until it came to a crate filled with plastic tiles. When it struck there, the doll was hurled several feet and its head came off, to continue bouncing on down along the hall.

"No! No!"

Panting, she snatched up the body and pursued the head.

"Be all right," she said when she had retrieved it. "Be all right."

But she could not get the head to go back on again. Clutching them together, she ran to the room with the closed door and opened it.

"Daddy!" she said. "Daddy! Daddy fix!"

The room was empty, dim, disorderly. She climbed up onto the unmade bed, seating herself in its middle.

"Gone away," she said, cradling the doll in her lap. "Be all right. Please be all right."

She held the head in place and watched it through moist prisms which formed without sobs. The rest of the room came to seem so much darker.

The cow dozed, head depressed, beside the tree where she was tethered. In his cart, Tibor ruminated: Where then is the elation? My dream, the substance of my masterpiece, my life's work—is almost within reach. It would have been so much more joyous a thing had He not appeared to me and done the things that He did. Now that I am assured the chance to frame Him in my art, the landscape of my joy divides and leaves me, not so dark as a silent house, but so confused, with my life gigantic, ripening to the point of bursting, with fear and ambition the last things left. To change it all to stone and stars—yes, I must try. Only, only now, it will be harder than I thought it would. That I still have that strength, that I still have it . . .

"Pete," he said, as the other came into the camp, Toby at his heels, tail a-wag. "How was your walk?"

"Pleasant," Pete said. "It's a nice night."

"I think there is a little wine left," Schuld said. "Why don't we all have a drink and finish it off?"

"All right. Let's."

He passed the bottle among them.

"The last of the wine," he said, disposing of the empty flask over his shoulder and into the trees. "No bread left either. How long till the day when the last of you must say that, Pete? Whatever made you choose the career that you did, times being what they are?"

Pete shrugged.

"Hard to say. Obviously, it wasn't a matter of popularity. Why does anyone choose anything and let it dominate his life? Looking for some sort of truth, I suppose, some form of beauty . . ."

"Don't forget goodness," Schuld said.

"That, too."

"I see. Aquinas cleaned up the Greeks for you, so Plato is okay. Hell, you even baptized Aristotle's bones, for that matter, once you found a use for his thoughts. Take away the Greek logicians and the Jewish mystics and you wouldn't have much left."

"We count the Passion and the Resurrection for something," Pete said.

"Okay. I left out the Oriental mystery religions. And for that matter, the Crusades, the holy wars, the Inquisition."

"You've made your point," Pete said. "I am weary of

these things and have trouble enough with the way my own mind works. You want to argue, join a debating team.

Schuld laughed.

"Yes, you are right. No offense meant, I assure you. I know your religion has troubles enough on the inside. No sense to dredging after more."

"What do you mean?"

"To quote a great mathematician, Eric Bell, 'All creeds tend to split into two, each of which in turn splits into two more, and so on, until after a certain finite number of generations (which can be easily calculated by logarithms) there are fewer human beings in any given region, no matter how large, than there are creeds, and further attenuations of the original dogma embodied in the first creed dilute it to a transparent gas too subtle to sustain faith in any human being, no matter how small.' In other words, you are falling apart on your own. Every little settlement across the land has its own version of the faith."

Pete brightened.

"If that is truly a natural law," he said, "then it applies across the board. The SOWs will suffer its effects just as we do. Only we have a tradition born of two thousand years' experience in weathering its operation. I find that encouraging."

"But supposing," Schuld said, "just supposing—what if the SOWs are right and you are wrong? What if there is really a divine influence acting to suspend this law for them? What then?"

Pete bowed his head, raised it, and smiled again.

"It is as the Arabs say, 'If it is the will of God it comes to pass.'"

"Allah," Schuld corrected.

"What's in a name? They differ from country to country."

"That is true. And from generation to generation. For that matter, given one more generation, everything may be different. Even the substance."

"Possibly," Pete said, rising to his feet. "Possibly. You have just reminded me that my bladder is brimming. Excuse me."

As Pete headed off into the bushes, Tibor said, "Perhaps it was better not to antagonize him so. After all, it may just make him more difficult to deal with when the times comes to distract him or mislead him or whatever you have in mind for when we find Lufteufel."

"I know what I am doing," Schuld said. "I want to demonstrate how tenuous, how misguided, a thing it is that he represents."

"I already know that you know more about religion than he does," Tibor said, "being head of your whole church and all, and him just a trainee. You don't have to show me that. I'd just as soon the rest of the trip went pleasantly and that we were all friends."

Schuld laughed.

"Just wait and watch," he said. "You will see that everything turns out properly."

This is not at all the way that I envisaged this Pilg, Tibor thought. I wish that I could have done it alone, found Lufteufel by myself, taken his likeness without fuss or bother, gone back to Charlottesville and finished my work. That is all. I have a great aversion to disputes of any kind. Now this, here, with them. I don't want to take sides. My feelings are with Pete, though. He didn't start it. I don't want a lesson in theology at his expense. I wish that it would just stop.

Pete returned.

"Getting a bit nippy," he said, stooping to toss more sticks onto the fire.

"It is just you," Schuld said, "feeling the outer darkness pressing in upon you, finally."

"Oh, for Christ's sake!" Pete said, straightening. "If you're so damn gone on that dippy religion, why don't you join it? Go bow down before the civil servant who gave the order that screwed things up! Model plaster busts of him from Tibor's murch! Play bingo at his feet! Hold raffles and Day of Wrath benefit picnics, too, while you're at it! You've still got a lot to learn, and that will all come later. But in the meantime, I just plain don't give a shit!"

Schuld roared with laughter.

"Very good, Pete! Very good!" he said. "I'm glad the rigor mortis has left your tongue intact. And you've reminded me of something I must go do now myself."

Schuld trudged off into the bushes, still chuckling.

"Damn that man!" Pete said. It is hard to keep recalling that he saved my life and that love is the name of the game. What has gotten into him that he is becoming my cross for today! That air-cooled, fuel-injection system with its absolutely balanced compression and exhaust cycle now seems aimed at running me down, backing over the remains to make it a perfect squash and leaving me there as flat and decorative as Tibor's murch. I am just going to refuse to talk to him if he starts in again.

"Why did he get that way all of a sudden?" Pete said, half to himself.

"I think that he has something against Christianity," Tibor said.

"I never would have guessed. Funny, though. He told me religion doesn't mean much to him."

"He did? That is strange, isn't it?"

"How do you see what he was talking about, Tibor?"

"Sort of the way you do," Tibor said. "I don't think I give a shit either."

Then they heard the howl, ending in a brief, intense yelp and a very faint whine. Then nothing.

"Toby!" Tibor screamed, activating the battery-powered circuit and driving his cart in the direction of the cry. "Toby!"

Pete spun about, raced to catch up with him. The cart broke through a stand of bushes, pushed past the gnarled hulk of a tree.

"Toby . . ." he heard Tibor say, as the cart screeched to a halt. Then, "You—killed—him—"

"Any other response would not have been personally viable," he heard Schuld's voice reply. "I maintain a standard reactive posture of nullification against subhuman forms which transgress. It's a common experience with me, this challenge. They detect my—"

Flailing, the extensor lashed out like a snapped cable and caught Schuld across the face. The man stumbled back catching hold of a tree. He drew himself erect then. His helmet had been knocked to the ground. Rolling, it had come to a halt beside the body of the dog, whose neck was twisted back at an unnatural angle. As Pete struggled to push his way through the brush, he saw that Schuld's lip had opened again and blood fell from his mouth, running down his chin, dripping. The head wound he had mentioned was also visible now, and it too began to darken moistly. Pete froze at the sight, for it was ghastly in the half-shadows and the ever-moving light from the fire. Then he realized that Schuld was looking at him. In that moment, an absolute hatred filled him, and he breathed the words, "I know you!" involuntarily. Schuld smiled and nodded, as if waiting for something.

But then Tibor, who had also been watching, wailed, "Murderer!" and the extensor snapped forward once more, knocking Schuld to the ground.

"No, Tibor!" Pete screamed, the vision broken, "Stop!"

Schuld sprang to his feet, half of his face masked

with blood, the more-human half wary now, wide-eyed and twisting toward fear. He turned and began to run.

The extensor snaked after, took a turn about his feet, tightened and lifted, sending him sprawling once more.

The cart creaked several feet forward and Pete raced about it.

By the time he reached the front, Schuld had risen to his knees, his face and breast a filthy, bloody abomination.

"No!" Pete shouted again, rushing to interpose himself between Tibor and his victim.

But the extensor was faster. It fell once more, knocking Schuld over backward.

Pete rushed to straddle the fallen man and raised his arms before Tibor.

"Don't do it, Tibor!" he cried. "You'll kill him! Do you hear me! You can't do it! For the love of God, Tibor! He's a man! Like you and me! It's murder! Don't—"

Pete had braced himself for the blow, but it did not come. Instead, the extensor plunged in from his left and the manual gripper seized hold of his forearm. The cart creaked and swayed at the strain, but Pete was raised into the air—three, four feet above the ground. Then, suddenly, the extensor moved like a cracking whip and he was hurled toward a clump of bushes. He heard Schuld's moaning as he fell.

He was scratched and poked, but not severely jolted, as the shrubs collapsed to cushion him. He heard the cart creaking again. Then, for several moments, he was unable to move, tangled and enmeshed as he was. As he struggled to free himself, he heard a bubbly gasp, followed by a rasping, choking sound.

Tearing at the twigs and limblets, he was finally able to sit up and behold what Tibor had done.

The extensor was projected out and up, rigid now as

a steel pole. Higher above the ground than Pete himself had dangled, hung Schuld, the gripper tight about his throat. His eyes and his tongue protruded. The veins in his forehead stood out like cords. Even as Pete stared, his limbs completed their *Totentanz,* fell slack, hung limp.

"No," Pete said softly, realizing that it was already too late, that there was nothing at all that he could do.

Tibor, I pray that you never realize what you have done, he thought, raising his hand to cover his eyes, for he was unable to close them or move them. It was planned, Tibor, planned down to the last detail. Except for this. Except for this . . . It was me. Me that he wanted. Wanted to kill him. Him. At the last moment, the very last moment, he would have shouted. Shouted out to you, Tibor. Shouted, "Ecce! Ecce! Ecce!" And you would have known, you would have felt, you would have beheld, as he desired, planned, required, the necessary death, at my hands, of Carleton Lufteufel. Hanging there, now, all blood and dirt, with eyes that look straight out, forever, across the surface of the world— he wanted me to do that for him, to him, with you to bear witness, here and forever, here and in the great murch in Charlottesville, to bear witness to all the world of the transfiguration of a twisted, tormented being who desired both adoration and punishment, worship and death—here revealed, suddenly, as I slew him, here transfigured, instantly, for you, for all the world, at the moment of his death—the Deus Irae. And God! It could have happened that way! It could have. But you are blinded now with madness and with hate, my friend. May they take this vision with them when they go, I pray. May you never know what you have done. May you never. May you never. Amen.

SEVENTEEN

Rain . . . A gray world, a chill world: Idaho. Basque country. Sheep. Jai alai. A language they say the Devil himself could not master . . .

Pete trudged beside the creaking cart. Thank the Lord it was not difficult, he thought, to convince Tibor that Lufteufel's place was nowhere near the spot Schuld had said it was. Two weeks. Two weeks, and Tibor is still hurting. He must never know how close he really was. He sees Schuld now as a madman. I wish that I could, too. The most difficult thing was the burial. I should have been able to say something, but I was as dumb as that girl with the broken doll in her lap we passed the next day, seated there at the crossroads. I should have managed some sort of prayer. After all, he was a man, he had an immortal soul. . . . Empty, though, my mouth. My lips were stuck together. We go on . . . A necessary errand of fools. So long as Tibor can be made to feel that Lufteufel is still somewhere ahead, we must go on. Forever, if it comes to that, looking for a man who is already dead. It was Tibor's fault, too, to think that God's vision could indeed be captured, to believe that a mortal artist could daub an epiphany with his colors. It was wrong, it was presumption of the highest order. Yet . . . He needs me now more than ever, shaken as he is. We must go on . . . where? Only God knows. The destination is no longer important. I cannot leave him, and he cannot go back— He chuckled. "Empty-handed" was the wrong term.

"What's funny?" Tibor said, up on the cart.

"Us."

"Why?"

"We haven't the sense to get out of the rain."

Tibor snorted. Proper as he was, he commanded a somewhat better view than Pete.

"If that is all that concerns you, I see a building down the hill. It looks like part of a barn. We may be nearing a settlement. There seems to be something more in the distance."

"Let's head for the barn," Pete said.

"We are already soaked. Can't get any wetter."

"This isn't doing your cart any good."

"That is true. All right. The barn."

"A painter named Wyeth liked scenes like that," Pete said when the shelter came into his view, hoping to route Tibor's thoughts away from his brooding. "I saw some of his pictures in a book once."

"Rainscapes?"

"No. Barns. Country stuff."

"Was he good?"

"I think so."

"Why?"

"His pictures looked exceptionally real."

"Real in what way?"

"The way things actually look."

Tibor laughed.

"Pete," he said, "there are an infinite number of ways of showing how things actually look. They are all of them right, because they show it. Yet each artist goes about it differently. It is partly what you choose to emphasize and partly how you do it. It is plain that you have never painted."

"True," Pete said, ignoring the water running down

his neck, pleased to have gotten Tibor talking on a subject that held more than a little of his attention. Then a peculiar thought struck him.

"Such being the case," he said suddenly, "if—when we find Lufteufel, how will you fulfill your commission honestly, properly, if there are an infinite number of ways you might go about it? Emphasis means showing one thing at the expense of another. How will you get a true portrait that way?"

Tibor shook his head vigorously.

"You misunderstood me. There are all those ways of doing it, but only one is the best."

"How do you know which one it is?" Pete asked.

Tibor was silent for a time. Then, "You just do," he said. "It feels—appropriate."

"I still don't understand."

Tibor was silent again.

"Neither do I," he finally said.

Inside the barn there was straw. Pete unhitched the cow and she munched it. He closed the door. He lay back in the straw and listened to the rain.

God! I'm tired! It has been a long pair of weeks, he thought. Haven't called Abernathy since right after it happened. Nothing new to say, though. Go on, he told me. Do not let Tibor know. Lead him through the land. Continue to search. My prayers go with you. Good night.

It was the only way. He saw that clearly now. There was a sweetish smell to the damp straw. A tangle of stiff leather hung from a nail overhead. Rain dripped from several holes in the roof. A rusted machine occupied a far corner. Pete thought of the beetles and the Great C extension, of the autofac and the twisted trail from Charlottesville; he thought of the card game that night, with Tibor, Abernathy, and Lurine; and of Tibor's sud-

den grasping at the faith; he thought of Lurine; he recalled his vision of Deity above the hook, and as suddenly that of the lidless-eyed regarder of the world and
all in it; Lufteufel, then, hung high, dark, hideous in his
ultimate frustration; he thought of Lurine. . . .

He realized that he had been asleep. The rain had
stopped. He heard Tibor's snores. The cow was chewing
her cud. He stretched. He scratched himself and sat up.

Tibor watched the shadows among the overhead
beams. If he had not taken back the arms and legs, he
thought, I could never have killed that strange man,
that hunter, that Jack Schuld. He was too strong. Only
the manipulators could have served. Why leave me with
the devices that would help me kill? For a while things
seemed to be going so well. . . . It seemed as if everything were near to completion, as if a few days more
would have seen a successful end to the Pilg. It seemed
as if the image might soon be captured and the job finished. I had—hope. Then, so quickly after . . . despair.
Is that an aspect of the God of Wrath? Perhaps Pete
raised a valid question. What to emphasize in such a
study? Even if I am to look upon his face, is it possible
that, this time, I may be unable to do a painting correctly? How can I capture the essence of such a being in
surface and color? It—it passeth understanding. . . . I
miss Toby. He was a good dog. I loved him. But that
poor madman—I am sorry I killed him. He could not
help it that he was mad. If I had kept those arms and
legs the whole thing would have been different. . . . I
might have given up and walked home. After all, I am
not even certain I could paint with real hands. God, if
you ever want to give them back, though . . . No, I do
not think I will ever have them again. It— I do
not understand. I was wrong in accepting this com-

mission. I am certain of that now. I wanted to depict that which may not be shown, that which cannot be understood. It is an impossible job. Pride. There is nothing else to me other than my skill. I know that I am good. It is all that I have, though, and I have made too much of it. I had felt, somehow, that it was more than sufficient, not just to make me the equal of a whole man, but to surpass other men, to surpass even the human. I wanted all the future generations of worshipers to look at that work and to see this. It was not the God of Wrath I wanted them to look upon with awe, but the skill of Tibor McMasters. I wanted that awe, their wonder, their admiration—their worship. I wanted deification through my art, I see that now. My pride brought me the entire way. I do not know what I am going to do now. —Go on, go on, of course. I must do that. This is not at all how I thought things might turn out.

The rain had stopped. He tensed and relaxed his muscles. He looked up. The cow was chewing her cud. He heard Pete's snores. No. Pete was sitting up, looking his way.

"Tibor?" Pete said.

"Yes?"

"Where is that snoring coming from?"

"I don't know. I thought it was you."

Pete stood, listening. He looked about the barn, turned, and moved toward a stall. He looked within. He would have dismissed it as a bundle of rags and trash if it had not been for the snoring. He leaned nearer and was engulfed by the aura of wine fumes which surrounded it. He drew back quickly.

"What is it?" Tibor called out.

"Some bum," Pete said, "sleeping one off, I think."

"Oh. Maybe he could tell us about the settlement up ahead. He might even know something more. . . ."

"I doubt that," Pete said. Holding his breath, he returned and examined the figure more closely: an untrimmed beard stained a number of colors, ancient crumbs of food still trapped within it, a glistening line of saliva down through its strands, framing teeth which had gone beyond yellow to a brownish cast, several of them broken, many missing, the remainder worn; the heavily lined face could be seen as sallow in the light which fell upon it through the nearest hole in the roof; nose broken at least twice; heavy encrustations of pus at the corners of the eyes, dried upon the lashes; hair wiry, tangled long and gray pale as smoke. A tension of pain lay upon that face even in sleep, so that tics, twitches, and sudden tightnesses animated it unnaturally, as though swarms of insects moved beneath the skin, fighting, breeding, dying. Over-all, the form was thin, wasted, dehydrated. "An old drunk," Pete said, turning back again. "That's all. Can't know too much about the settlement. They probably ran him out of it."

The rain has stopped and there is still some light, Pete thought. Best we leave him here and get moving again. Whatever he has to tell us will hardly be worth the hearing, and we would be stuck with a hangover bum on our hands.

"Let's just leave him and go," he told Tibor.

As he moved away, the man moaned and muttered, "Where are you?"

Pete was silent.

"Where are you?" came the croaking voice once more, followed by a thrashing about from within the stall.

"Maybe he is ill," Tibor said.

"I do not doubt it."

"Come here," said the voice, "come here . . ."

Pete looked at Tibor.

"Maybe there is something we can do," Tibor said. Pete shook his head, moved back to the stall.

Just as he looked about the partition, the man said, "There you are," but he was not looking at Pete. He was addressing a jug he had withdrawn from beneath a mound of straw. He uncorked it but lacked the strength to raise it to his lips. He threw his head back then and turned it to the side. He tipped the jug toward his mouth, sucked upon it. Some of the wine splashed over his face. As he uprighted the jug, he was seized with a spell of coughing. Ragged, breaking sounds emerged from his chest, his throat, his mouth. When he spat, Pete could not tell whether it was blood or wine residue that reddened the spittle so. Pete moved to withdraw.

"I see you," the man said suddenly, his voice slightly firmer than it had been. "Don't go away. Help old Tom." His voice slid into a practiced whine then. "Please, mister, can you spare a—help? A help for me? M'arms don't work so good. Must've slept on 'em funny."

"What do you want?" Pete asked.

"Hold this jug for me, please. I don't want to spill any."

"All right," Pete said.

Holding his breath, he entered the stall and knelt beside the old man. He raised the frail shoulders with his right arm, gripped the jug with his left hand. "Here," he said, and he held it tilted while the other drew a long series of swallows from it.

"Thank you," said the man, coughing less vigorously than before, but still showering Pete's wrist and forearm.

Pete lowered him quickly and set down the jug. He began to draw away, but a bony hand snatched his wrist.

"Don't go, don't go. I'm Tom, Tom Gleason. Where you from?"

"Utah. Charlottesville, Utah," Pete said, struggling not to breathe.

"Denver," said Tom, "that's all, thank you. It was a nice city. Good people, you know? Someone always had the price of a flop and—what's the word? Thunderbird!" He chuckled. "What's the price? Thirty twice. You want a drink, mister? You have some of this. Ain't bad. Found it in the cellar of an old place off the road, back—" His hand flopped. "What way? Oh hell! There's more there. Have some. Still plenty here."

"Thanks," Pete said. "No."

"You ever been to Denver?"

"No."

"Remember how nice it was before they burned it. The people were nice, you know? They—"

Pete exhaled, breathed, gagged.

"Yeah, gets me that way, too," Tom said. "Burning a nice place like that. Why'd they do it, anyhow?"

"It was a—war," Pete said. "Cities get bombed when you have wars."

"I didn't want no war. It was such a nice place. No reason to bomb a nice place like Denver. I got burned when they did it." His hand plucked feebly at his tattered shirt. "Want to see my scars?"

"That's all right."

"I got 'em. Got plenty. Had me in a field hospital for a while. Threw me out soon as I got better. It wasn't nice anymore. Hardly anything to drink, or eat either. Those was rough times. I don't remember so much anymore, but I went a lot of places after that. Nothing left like Denver was, though. Nothing nice left. People ain't so nice anymore either, you know? Hard to get a little juice from folks nowadays. —Sure you don't want none?"

"Better save it," Pete said. "Hard to get."

"That's the truth. Help me to another, will you?"

"Okay."

While he was doing this, Tibor called out, "How is he?"

Pete said, "Coming around." Then, "Wait awhile."

On an impulse then, he asked Tom, "Do you know who Carleton Lufteufel was?"

The old man looked at him blankly, shook his head.

"Might have heard the name. Might not. Don't remember so well anymore. Friend . . . ?"

"Just a name to me, too," Pete said. "But I've got a friend here—a poor little inc, who has been looking all over for him. Probably, he'll never find him. Probably, he'll just go on and on and die looking."

Tom's eyes brimmed over.

"Poor little inc," he said, "poor little inc . . ."

"Can you say the name?" Pete asked.

"What name?"

"Carleton Lufteufel."

"Gimme another drink, please."

Pete held him again.

"Now?" he said. "Now can you say Carleton Lufteufel?"

"Carleton Lufteufel," Tom said. "I can still talk. Just my memory that's bad . . ."

"Would you—" No, it was ridiculous. Tibor would see right through it. Or would he? Pete wondered. Tom Gleason was about the right age. Tibor already thought he was ill, knew he had been drinking. And more important, perhaps, Tibor's faith in his own judgment seemed to have waned since the killing of Schuld/Lufteufel. If I act convinced, Pete thought, will it be enough of an extra push to make him believe? If I act convinced and Tom states it for a fact? We could go on forever, wandering, looking, without another opportunity like this, a chance to return to Charlottesville, to finish my studies, to see Lurine again. And if I could succeed, think of the irony! Think of the Servants of Wrath bowing down, praying to, venerating, adoring, not their god in the form of Carleton Lufteufel, but one of his victims: a worthless derelict, a drunken brain-scarred old drifter, a panhandler, a wino, a man—a man who had never done anything to or for his fellows, a maimed human cipher who had never wielded power of any sort; just a man, at his lowest. Think of him in the SOWs' place of honor! I have to try.

"Would you do a kindness for my poor little inc friend?" he asked.

"Do a what? A kindness? God, yes . . . There's enough misery in the world. If it's not too hard, that is. I'm not the man I used to be. What's he want?"

"He wants to see Carleton Lufteufel, a man we will never find. All that he wants to do is take his picture. Would you—would you say that you are Carleton Lufteufel, that you were once Chairman of the ERDA? And if he asks you, that you gave the bomb order? That's all. Would you do it? Can you?"

"One more drink," Tom said.

Pete raised him to the jug.

"Is everything all right?" Tibor called out.

"Yes," Pete called back. "This may be very important! We may have had a stroke of luck, if I can get this fellow back into shape. . . . Hold on!"

He lowered the jug. Tom eased away from his arm and sat unassisted. And then, by degrees, his eyes shut. He had passed out. Either that, or—god forbid; he was dead.

"Tom," Pete said.

Silence. And the inertness of a million years: something below the level of life, something still inanimate which had never made it up to sentience. And probably never would.

Shit, Pete Sands thought. He took the bottle of wine, put the screw-type lid back on it, sat for a time. "The piece of luck I was talking about," he called loudly. "Do you believe at all in destiny?"

"What?" Tibor yelled back, with signs of irritation.

Reaching into his pocket, Pete Sands got out his roll of silver dimes, always kept there. The all-purpose winning possession, he thought; he got a good grip on the roll of dimes and then tapped it against Tom's cheekbone. Nothing. No response. Pete then tore the heavy brown-paper wrapper away from the dimes. The metal coins slithered and tinkled against one another, manifesting themselves into visibility.

"Carleton Lufteufel," ol' Tom muttered, eyes still shut. "That poor little inc. I wouldn't want the poor blighted inc wandering till he got hurt. It's a rough world out there, you know?" Ol' Tom opened his eyes; they were clear and lucid as he surveyed the many dimes in Pete's palm. "Chairman of the ERDA, whatever that is—and I gave the bomb order, if the inc asks me. Okay; I got it straight. Carleton Lufteufel, that's me." He coughed and spat again, ran his fingers through his hair. "You wouldn't have a comb, would you? If I'm going to have my picture took—" He held out his hand. Pete gave him the dimes. All of them.

"Afraid not," Pete said.

"You help me up then. Carleton Lufteufel, ERDA, bomb order if he asks." Ol' Tom put the dimes away, out of sight; all at once they were gone. As if they had never been.

Pete said loudly, "This is extraordinary. You think there's a supernatural entity which guides men along every step of their lives? You think that, Tibor? I never thought so, not before. But my god. I have been talking with this man since he woke up. He is not well, but then he has been through a lot." He prodded Tom Gleason. "Tell my friend who you are," he said.

Tom showed a broken-toothed smile. "Name's Carleton Lufteufel."

Tibor gasped. "Are you joking?"

"Wouldn't joke about my own name now, son. A man might use a lot of them in a lot of different places. But at a time like this, when someone's been looking so hard for me, there's no point in denying it. Yes, I'm Carleton Lufteufel. I used to be Chairman of the ERDA."

Tibor stared at him without moving.

"I gave the bomb order," the old man added, then.

Tibor continued to stare.

Tom appeared a trifle uneasy, but held his ground, held his smile.

But the moments passed, and Tibor still did not respond. Finally Tom's face slackened.

A little longer; then, "You ever been in Denver?"

"No," Tibor said.

Pete wanted to scream, but then Tom said, "It was a nice city. Pretty. Good people. Then came the war. They burned it, you know. . . ." His face underwent contortions and his eyes glistened.

"I was Chairman of the ERDA. I gave the bomb order," he said again.

Tibor's head moved and his tongue licked over the control unit. An extensor moved, activating a stereo, full-color, wide-angle, tel-scope, fast-action, shirtbutton-sized war-surplus camera the Servants of Wrath had provided him for this purpose.

I will never know the best way, Tibor thought. I will never do the perfect job with a subject like this. But then it does not matter. I will do the best that I can, the best that I can to show this subject as he is, to give them their murch, as they want it, to glorify their god, as they would see him glorified, not to my greater honor and glory, or even to his, but simply to fulfill this commission, as I promised. Whether it was destiny or simply luck does not matter. Our journey is over. The Pilg has been completed. I have his likeness. What can I say to him now that this is done?

"I'm pleased to meet you," Tibor said. "I just took your picture. I hope that is all right with you."

"Sure, son, sure. Glad to be of help. I'm going to have to get back to rest now, though, if your friend here will give me a hand. I'm ailing, you know."

"Is there anything we could do?"

"No, thanks. I've got plenty of medicine laid by. You're nice people. Have a good trip."

"Thank you, sir."

Tom flipped one hand at him, as Pete caught his arm and steered him back to the stall.

Home! Tibor thought, his eyes filling with tears. We can go home now. . . .

He waited for Pete to come and harness the cow.

That night they sat by a small fire Pete had kindled. The clouds had blown over and the stars shone in the fresh-washed sky. They had eaten dry rations. Pete had found a half jar of instant coffee in an abandoned farmhouse. It was stale, but it was hot and black and steamed attractively under the breeze from the south.

"There were times," Tibor said, "when I thought I would never make it."

Pete nodded.

"Still mad I came along?" he asked.

Tibor chuckled.

"Go on, push your advantage," he said. ". . . Hell of a way to get converts."

"Are you still going Christian?"

"Still thinking about it. Let me finish this job first."

"Sure." Pete had tried to get through to Abernathy earlier, but the storm system had blanked him out. No hurry now though, he thought. It is all right. Over.

"Want to see his picture again?"

"Yes."

Tibor's extensor moved, withdrew the picture from its case, passed it down to him.

Pete studied Tom Gleason's tired, old features. Poor guy, he thought. May be dead by now. Not a thing we could have done for him, though. What if—? Supposing it was no coincidence? Supposing it was something more than luck that gave him to us? The irony I saw in Lufteufel's victim deified . . . Could it run deeper even than irony? He turned the picture, looking into the eyes, a bit brighter for the moment as the man had realized he was making someone happy, a touch of pain in the lowering, the tightening of the brows as he had recalled his nice Denver gone. . . .

Pete drank his coffee, passed the picture back to Tibor.

"You don't seem unhappy," Tibor said, "that the competition is getting what it wants."

Pete shrugged.

"It's not that big a thing to me," he said. "After all, it's only a picture."

Tibor replaced it in his case.

"Did he look the way you thought he would?" he asked.

Pete nodded, thinking back over faces he had known.

"Pretty much," he said. "Have you decided how you will handle it?"

"I'll give them a good job. I know that."

"More coffee?"

"Thanks."

Tibor extended his cup. Pete filled it, added some to

his own. He looked up at the stars then, listened to the noises of the night, breathed the warm wind—how warm it had become!—and sipped the coffee.

"Too bad I didn't find some cigarettes, too."

EIGHTEEN

At the side of the dust-run serving as a road, the cretin girl Alice remained in silence, and a thousand years passed as sun came and day held a time and finally fell into darkness. She knew he was dead, even before the lizzy approached her.

"Miss."

She did not look up.

"Miss, come along with us."

"No!" she said, violently.

"The cadaver—"

"I no *want!*"

Seating itself beside her, the lizzy said in a patient voice, "By custom you're supposed to claim it." Time passed; she kept her eyes shut, so as not to see, and with her hands over her ears she could not be certain if it was speaking further or not. At last it touched her on the shoulder. "You're a *re*tard, aren't you?"

"No."

"You're too retarded to know what I'm saying. He's dressed as a hunter, but he's the old man you were shacking up with, the rat man. He is the rat man, isn't he? Disguised. What was he doing disguised? Trying to get away from enemies, was he?" The lizzy laughed roughly, then, the scales of its body ambient in the noise of its voice. "Didn't work. They bashed his face in. You should see it; nothing but pulp and—"

She leaped up and ran, then ran back for her forgotten doll. The lizzy had the doll, and the lizzy grinned at her, not giving the doll to her but pressing it against its scaly chest. Mockery of her.

"He good man!" she shouted frantically, as she scrabbled for the doll, her doll.

"No, he wasn't a good man. He wasn't even a good rat catcher. A lot of times, more than you know, he sold old gristly rats for the price supposed to be the going rate for young plump ones. What did he used to do, before he was a rat catcher?"

Alice said, "Bombs."

"Your daddy."

"Yes, my daddy."

"Well, since he was your daddy we'll bring you the corpse. You stay here." The lizzy rose, dropped the doll before her, and ambulated off, after its fashion.

Seated by the doll, she watched the lizzy go, feeling the tears running silently down her cheeks. Knew it wouldn't work, she thought. Knew they'd get him. Maybe for bad rats; tough old ones . . . like it just now said.

Why is it all like this? she wondered. He gave me this doll, a long time ago. Now he won't give me nothing more again. Ever. Something is wrong, she realized. But why? People, they are here for a time and then even if you love them they are gone and it is for always, they are never back, not now.

Once more she shut her eyes and sat rocking back and forth.

When again she looked, a man who wasn't a lizard was coming along the dust-rut road toward her. It was her daddy. As she leaped up joyfully she realized that something had happened to him, and she faltered, taken aback by the transformation in him. Now he stood straighter, and his face had a kindness glowing about it, a warm expression, without the twistedness she had become accustomed to.

Her daddy approached, step by step, in a certain measured fashion, as if in solemn dance toward her, and then he seated himself silently, indicating to her to be seated, too. It was odd, she thought, that he did not speak, that he only gestured. There was about him a peacefulness she had never witnessed before, as if time had rolled back for him, making him both younger and—more gentle. She liked him better this way; the fear she had always felt toward him began to leave her, and she reached out, haltingly, to touch his arm.

Her fingers passed through his arm. And it came to her, then, in an instant, in a twinkling of an eye, a flash of insight, that this was only his spirit, that as the lizzy had said, her daddy was dead. His spirit had stopped on its way back to be with her, to spend a final moment resting by the side of the road with her. This was why he did not speak. Spirits could not be heard.

"Can you hear me?" she asked.

Smiling, her daddy nodded.

An unusual sense of understanding things began to course through her, a kind of alertness which she could not recall from any time ever. It was as if a . . . she struggled for the word. A membrane of some nature had been removed from her mind; she could see in the sense that she could comprehend now what she had never comprehended. Gazing around her, she saw in truth, in very truth, a different world, a world comprehensible at last, even if only for an interval.

"I love you," she said.

Again he smiled.

"Will I see you again?" she asked him.

He nodded.

"But I have to—" She hesitated, because these were difficult thoughts. "Pass across first, before that time."

Smiling, he nodded.

"You feel better, don't you," she said. It was evident beyond any doubt, from every aspect of him. "What is gone from you is something terrible," she said. Until now, now that it had gone, she had never understood how dreadful it was. "It was an evil about you. Is that why you feel better? Because now the evil about you—"

Rising silently to his feet, her daddy began to move away, along the dim marks of the road.

"Wait," she said.

But he could not or would not wait. He continued on away, now, his back to her, growing smaller, smaller, and then at last he disappeared; she watched him go and then she saw what remained of him travel through a clump of tangled rubbish and debris—*through*, not around, ghostly and pale as he had become; he did not step aside to avoid it. And he had become very small, now, only three or so feet high, fading and sinking, dwindling into bits of mere light which drifted suddenly away in swirls which the wind carried off, and were absorbed by the day.

Two lizzys came toiling along toward her, both of them looking perplexed and somewhat angry.

"It's gone," the first lizzy said to her. "Your corpse is gone—your father's, I mean."

"Yes," Alice said. "I know."

"It was stolen, I guess," the other lizzy said. Half to itself it added, "Something dragged it off . . . maybe ate it."

Alice said, "It rose."

"It what?" Both lizzys stared at her, and then simultaneously they broke into laughter. "Rose from the dead? How do you know? Did it come floating by here?"

"Yes," she said. "And stayed a moment to sit with me."

Cautiously, one lizzy said to its companion, in a totally changed tone of voice, "A miracle."

"Just a *re*tard," the other said. "Prattling nonsense, like they do. Burned-out brain muttering. It was just a dead human, nothing more."

With genuine curiosity, the other lizzy asked the girl, "Where'd it go from here? Maybe we can catch up with it. Maybe it can tell the future and heal!"

"It dissipated," Alice said.

The lizzys blinked, and then one of them rustled its scales uneasily and muttered, "This is no retard; did you hear that word she used? Retards don't use words like that, not words like 'dissipated.' Are you sure this is the right girl?"

Alice, with her doll held tight, turned to go. A few of the particles of light which had comprised her daddy's transformed being brushed about her, like moonbeams visible in the day, like a magic, living dust spreading out across the landscape of the world, to become progressively finer and finer, always more rare, but never completely to disappear. At least not for her. She could still sense the bits, the traces, of him around her, in the air itself, hovering and lingering, and in a certain real sense, speaking a message.

And the membrane which had, all her life, occluded her mind—it remained gone. Her thoughts continued clear and distinct, and so they were to remain, for the rest of her life.

We have advanced up the manifold one move, she thought. My father and I . . . he beyond visible sight, and I into visible sight at last.

Around her the world sparkled in the warmth of day, and it seemed to her that it had permanently changed as well. What are these transformations? she asked herself. Certainly they will last; certainly they will endure. But she could not really be positive, because she had never witnessed anything like it before. In any case, what she perceived on all sides of her as she walked away from the puzzled lizards was good. Perhaps, she thought, it is springtime. The first spring since the war. She thought, The contamination is lifting from us all, finally, as well as from the place we live. And she knew why.

Dr. Abernathy felt the world's oppression lift but he did not have any insight as to why it had lifted. At the moment it began he had taken a walk to market for the purchase of vegetables. On the way back he smiled to himself, enjoying the air because it had—what was it once called?—he could not remember. Oh yes: ozone. Negative ions, he thought. The smell of new life. Associated with the vernal equinox; that which charged the Earth from solar flares, perhaps, from the great source.

Somewhere, he thought, a good event has happened, and it spreads out. He saw to his amazement palm trees. All at once he stopped, stood clasping his basket of string beans and beets. The warm air, the palm trees . . . funny, he thought, I never noticed any palm trees growing around here. And dry dusty land, as if I'm in the Middle East. Another world; touches of another continuum. I don't understand, he thought. What is breaking through? As if my eyes are now opened, in a special way.

To his right, a few people who had been shopping had seated themselves along the way, for rest. He saw young people, dusty from the walk, sweating, but full of a purity new to him. A pretty girl with dark hair, somewhat chubby, she had unfastened her shirt; it did not bother him; he was not offended by her naked breasts. The film is scrubbed away, he thought, and again he wondered why. A good deed done? Hardly. There was no such deed. He paused, standing there, admiring the young people, the bareness of the girl who did not seem self-conscious at all although she saw him, a Christian, gazing.

Somehow goodness has arrived, he decided. As Milton wrote once, "Out of evil comes good." Notice, he said to himself, the relative disparity of the two terms; evil is the most powerful term for what is bad, and good—it barely surpasses its opposite. The Fall of Satan, the Fall of Man, the crucifixion of Christ . . . out of those dreadful, evil acts came good; out of the Fall of Man and the expulsion from the Garden, man learned love. From a Trinity of Evil emerged at last a Trinity of Good! It is a balanced thing.

Then, he thought, possibly the world has been cleared of its oppressive film by an evil act . . . or am I getting into subtleties? In any case, he sensed the difference; it was real.

I swear to god I'm somewhere in Syria, he thought. In the Levant. Back in time, too, perhaps . . . thousands of years, possibly. He stood gazing around him, inhaling and excited, amazed.

To his right, the ruins of a prewar U. S. Post Office substation.

Old ruins, he thought. The antique world. Reborn, somehow, in this our present. Or have I been carried back? Not me back, he decided, but it transported in time, as through a weak spot, to enter here and suffuse us. Or me. Probably no one else sees it. My god, he thought, this is like Pete Sands and his drugs, except that I haven't taken anything. This is the sundering of the normal and the entry into or else the invasion by the paranormal which he experiences; this, he realized, is a vision, and I must try to fathom it.

He walked slowly across the stubble and dirt of the field, toward the ruins of the small U. S. Post Office substation. Against its standing wall lounged several people, enjoying midday rest and the sun. The sun! What vigor carried invisibly in its light, now!

They do not see what I see, he decided. Nothing is changed for them. *What happened to bring this on?* An ordinary sunny day in the world . . . if I interpret what I see as if it is mere symbol: a sunny day, representing in the highest order the termination of the authority of evil, of that obscure dominion? Yes, something evil has perished, he realized, and, understanding that, his heart gladdened.

Something of substance which was evil, he thought, has become only shadow. It has somehow lost an essential personification. *Did Tibor take the God of Wrath's picture, and in so doing steal his soul?*

He chuckled with delight, standing there by the ruins of the old U. S. Post Office substation, the sun radiating down on him, the fields murmuring with the buzz and drone of satisfaction, the mild endless hum of life. Well, he said to himself, amused, if Carleton Lufteufel's soul can be stolen, then he is not a god but a man, like any of the rest of us. Gods have nothing to fear from cameras. Except, he thought, pleased at his pun, a fear of (he laughed delightedly) exposure.

Several half-dozing people glanced up at him and smiled mildly, not knowing why he was laughing and yet sharing in it themselves.

More somberly, Dr. Abernathy thought, The Servants of Wrath may be with us for a long time—false religions are as long-lasting as the real, it would seem— but the reality of it has faded and fled from the world, and what remains is hollow and without the mekkis, the power, it had.

I will be interested in seeing the photograph which Tibor and Pete Sands bring back, he decided. As they say, Better a devil known.

By snaring his image they have broken him, he realized. They have reduced him to mortal size.

The palm trees rustled in the warm midday wind, acquainting him further, without words, in the sunny mystery of redemption. He was wondering, however, whom he could tell his pun to. *The false god,* he repeated in rapture, since normally he was very bad at jokes, *cannot survive exposure. He must always be concealed. We have lured him out and frozen his visage. And he is doomed.*

And so, he informed himself, by means of a project engineered by the guile and ambitions of the Servants of Wrath themselves, we Christians, evidently defeated, have triumphed; this portrait has initiated a process of perishing for him, by its very authenticity—or rather the fact that the Servants of Wrath will insist on its authenticity, collaborating in their own downfall. Thus the True God uses evil to refine the good, and good to refine evil, which is to say, in the final analysis we discover that God Himself has been served by everyone. By every event, whether good or bad.

I mean, he thought, *labeled* good or bad. Good or bad, truth or error, the wrong road or the right road, ignorance and malice and wisdom and love . . . they are, he thought, to be viewed as, *Omniae vitae ad Deum ducent.* All lives, like all roads, lead—not to Rome, but to God.

Walking on now, he reflected that he should put this in a sermon along with his pun; it was something to tell people, to make them smile as those resting persons by the ruins of the old U. S. Post Office substation had smiled. Even if they did not understand thoughts so complex, they could still take pleasure in them.

To enjoy things again . . . the world's oppression, vanquished by an act invisible to everyone, could not hold men back; they could bask and smile and unbutton their shirts to catch the sun and enjoy the humor of a simple priest.

I would like to know what did happen, he thought. But God occludes men to fulfill His will.

Maybe, Dr. Abernathy decided, it is better that way.

Firmly gripping his basket of string beans and beets, he continued on in the direction of Charlottesville and his little church.

NINETEEN

The murch which Tibor McMasters painted did slowly become known throughout the world and was at last rated as equal to the works of the great masters of the Italian Renaissance, most of which were known in the form of prints, the originals having been destroyed.

Seventeen years after Tibor's death, an official pronouncement of authentication was made by the Servants of Wrath hierarchy. It was indeed the visage of the God of Wrath, Carleton Lufteufel. There could be no doubt. Any disputing this was henceforth illegal and carried a penalty of emasculation for men, one ear removed for women. This was to insure reverence in an irreverent world, faith in a society which had become faithless, and belief in a world which had already discovered that most of what it believed were in actuality lies.

At the time of his death, Tibor was subsisting on a small annual pension from the Church, plus a guaranteed maintenance of his cart, with alfalfa hay for two cows: because of the excellence of his work he was given two cows, not one, to pull his cart. When he passed by, people recognized him and hailed him. He gave out a laborious autograph to tourists. Children yelled at him and did not jeer; Tibor was liked by everyone, and although he became eccentric and irascible in his old age, he was considered an asset to the community . . . this despite the fact that after rendering the true portrait of the God of Wrath he never painted anything of note again.

It was said that among his effects were certain diary-like entries he had jotted down from time to time, in which, to himself alone, he had expressed toward the end certain reservations as to the authenticity of his own great murch. However, no one saw such personal holo-graphs. If they existed at all, the Servants of Wrath who sequestered his corpus of papers either filed them away behind locked metal doors or, more likely, destroyed them.

His last two cows were killed and stuffed and placed, one on each side of his great murch, to gaze solemnly— and glassily—at the tourists who came to pay homage to the renowned painting. Tibor McMasters himself was finally made a saint of the Church. His grave site is unknown. Several cities proudly claim it.